Catching Up.....

By R. Pepe

To Cheri,
We live what we see!
Best always.
Kurt —

First published by Dog Ear Publishing
4010 W. 86th Street, Ste H
Indianapolis, IN 46268
www.dogearpublishing.net

dog ear
PUBLISHING

ISBN: 978-145750-600-0

This book is printed on acid-free paper.

This book is a work of fiction. Places, events, and situations in this book are purely fictional and any resemblance to actual persons, living or dead, is coincidental.

Printed in the United States of America

LIST OF CHAPTERS

TOMORROW Chapter 1
The Caller 3

EARLY 1940s Chapters 2–6
29 Crabtree Lane 9
The Circus..15
Walking Tall 27

SAYING GOOD-BYE Chapters 7–10
Deadly Affair 37
Best Man..43
Decisions 48

WHERE TO HIDE Chapters 11–14
The Nanny..61
The Red Rooster..69
The Photographer..76

STARTING OVER Chapters 15–21
New Friends...83
The Italians 95
Coast to Coast...110

TODAY Chapter 22
Bear in the Chair...125

TOMORROW

The Caller

.

1

KAREN COULDN'T BELIEVE that tomorrow would mark the fifth anniversary of the day she had shipped Mike's urn to his grieving family in Brooklyn so they could have a proper Italian wake. She was sure the urn had ended up in one of those 12 x 12 vaults with a glass front, displaying Mike's picture. Karen had had nothing to say about how things were handled. That was to be his family's decision, and she'd had no desire to intentionally hurt them further.

Mike's mother had suffered a mini stroke when she had been told that Mike's wife hadn't even had the decency to hold a memorial service for her beloved first-born. It was bad enough that Karen had dragged him off to the other end of the earth years before....not to mention the fact that Karen was unable to bear children to carry on the Mario family name.

When Karen had received the phone call from Memorial Hospital that her husband was in critical condition, her first thought had been, *Oh no, the Viagra must have lasted more than four hours.* They had said that she should come to the emergency room as quickly as possible.

After hanging up the phone, Karen had dug into the back of her junk drawer to find her emergency pack of cigarettes. She had pulled one out and headed for the deck to get her thoughts together. She had been preparing for this day for a long time and knew exactly what had to be done.

As she had entered the hospital, she had seen a clergyman walking toward her. She knew he was going to escort her to the special little room with only four chairs and a round table. Karen knew the drill. She was also sure the receptionist had hit the red button on the side of the desk to notify the doctor that she had arrived.

Within minutes, the doctor had joined them to express his sympathy. He explained how they had done everything possible to save Mike. Mike's death had been caused by massive injuries to his head, and given Mike's preexisting condition; he really didn't have a chance to survive the crash.

The police had suspected that Mike had been texting when his SUV hit the center divider and rolled over. "Is there anyone I can call for you?" the doctor had asked.

Karen had taken a deep breath, shook her head, and said, "No, but I do need twenty original copies of the death certificate."

When the clergyman had offered to escort Karen to the chapel, she had said it wasn't necessary. She truly believed that God knew exactly what He was doing. Mike had lived life to the fullest, always teeter-tottering on the edge. Most people who knew the real Mike had known it was only a matter of time before his lifestyle would catch up with him.

Mike had lived on borrowed time for a little more than two years. He and Karen had discussed his condition over and over again. No matter what threats she made, nothing would change his mind. He had spent his whole life in the drug business; there was no way he would ever take any medication. He had told Karen she needed to honor his decision and that, with the exception of Megan and Frank, no one was to know anything.

They had also discussed what needed to be done when Mike passed away. He had walked Karen through everything, step by step: his files, insurance policies, and bank statements, ending with a list of the people he wanted her to call. Mike had made Karen promise only one thing: "No memorial service. Send my ashes to Brooklyn and let my family do whatever they want." After the speech, he would always end with, "Don't worry, Karen, the only way I'll ever go to the hospital again is if the Viagra lasts more than four hours."

Halfway out the front door while lost in thoughts of that day, Karen heard the phone ring. Hesitating for only a minute, she went back inside to see who was calling. With so many things happening at this point in her life, when she looked at the caller ID and saw "Private Caller," she knew she had to answer it. After saying hello, she heard a voice that sounded familiar but that she could not place.

The next thing she remembered was seeing the phone batteries on the floor next to the phone. At this point, her whole body was trembling and tears were pouring down her cheeks. Stooping down to pick up the pieces, Karen saw Norman coming down the hall. In a very soft, calm voice, she said, "Mommy's not going out now. We need to have a talk. Get your stuff, and let's go upstairs on the big bed, okay?" Norman went over to his toy box and got his favorite stuffed bunny. As he headed toward the stairs, he turned, only once, to make sure Karen was right behind him.

When Karen finally got comfortable on the bed, Norman put his head in her lap and closed his eyes. He knew these sessions could go on for a long time. She always started each story the same way: If only Mike had had a chance to meet Norman, she was sure Mike would have loved him as much as she did. Then she would begin her story for that day.

When Mommy was a little girl, I went to stay at my grandmother's house during the summer. We had a lot of fun together. She let me help her make pies and cookies, took me on outings to the farms to pick berries and to the apple orchards to pick apples.

She always had lots of toys for me to play with. One year, I got the best gift in the world. When I arrived at my grandmother's house, I found a very soft big brown bear sitting on my bed, waiting for me. When I saw him, I was so excited that I put my arms around him and cried, "Oh Grandma, I love him. I am going to call him Mr. Bear." From that day on, he became my very best friend. I told him all my secrets, like I tell you now.

Every year, when I would return to my grandmother's house, he would be there, sitting in my little rocking chair where I left him, waiting to hear about my time away from him.

So, Norman, don't worry about Mommy; I am going to be okay. After almost thirty years, I will get to see Mr. Bear, tomorrow.

EARLY 1940s

29 Crabtree Lane
The Circus
Walking Tall

2

LEAVING THE AMUSEMENT park, Will Peterson had spotted her on the other side of the boardwalk. Maggie had been hanging over the railing, watching the incoming tide crashing against the jetty. Only minutes before, Will had given her a cone full of cotton candy and had half-jokingly asked her to marry him. Throwing her arms around his neck, she had replied only "When?"

Not certain if he was dreaming or actually living this night, Will had turned to his friend and said, "We're getting married." For Will, this had made it official.

Pulling into North Station, Will and Maggie Peterson felt like they were riding on a cloud rather than a train. Only yesterday they had tied the knot in a little chapel near Old Orchard Beach, where they had met. Now they were arriving in Boston to start their new life. After 20 years in the army, Will was finally going to have the life he had always wanted.

Leaving the station, Will hailed a taxi to take them to his studio apartment on Beacon Hill, where they would live until they found a house. Will had always known that he wanted to settle in one particular little town just outside of Boston. It was known for its excellent school systems and very low crime rate and was within easy commuting distance of his office. Also, everything you needed was within walking distance. Maggie would have preferred to stay in the city.

When the search for a home began, Will discovered that the prices were much higher than he had anticipated. After looking at several homes, he realized that it might be impossible to find one he could afford. He had only one house left to look at, and if that didn't work, he would have to rethink his plan.

As they went down Crabtree Lane, all Will and Maggie saw were old estate homes. When they saw the sign "House for sale," they didn't quite know what to make of it. This must be some mistake. The sale price listed in the paper could not be correct. Will decided to ring the bell and find out what the story was anyway.

When Walter Johnson opened the door, he explained that the house for sale was in the back of his property. Walter invited the Petersons into his home and introduced them to his wife, Harriet. He said that there was an interesting story attached to the house for sale and thought Will and Maggie might want to hear it before they looked at the house.

Walter went on to say that the original owner of the house had been named James Fitzgerald. James had decided to build a small house in the back of his property for his newly married daughter. In the end, he had given his daughter the big house and he and his wife had moved into the smaller one. A month after Old Man Fitzgerald's wife passed away, his daughter had found her father dead in the basement. The cause of his death had never been revealed.

Within a month, Fitzgerald's daughter and husband had moved away and put both houses up for sale. It was a package deal and at a very reasonable price. The houses had been vacant for more than a year before the Johnsons had bought them. They tried for many months to rent the little house, 29 Crabtree Lane, but had not been successful, so they had put it up for sale. No one in town, including the Johnsons' realtor, claimed to know anything about the history of the house.

The most important thing for Will and Maggie was that the price of the house was within their budget. They really didn't care how or why it was available. As they walked down a long driveway nestled in among the trees, they saw a pretty white house with a detached garage. On one side was a small yard with room for a garden. On the other side of the house was a two foot high brick wall to separate the two yards. From the front porch, they could see the Johnsons' entire backyard on one side and the backyard of the smaller house on the other.

It had everything Will and Maggie had hoped for, a living room, kitchen and two bedrooms on the first floor. A stairway off the kitchen led to a very large attic with two windows facing the driveway. Will knew that he could convert this into two bedrooms for his children. Two months later, the newlyweds moved into their new home.

They decided to make the larger bedroom theirs and the smaller bedroom Maggie's work room. The only thing she had ever wanted to do was to be a fashion designer and make the most elegant clothes women had ever seen. Maggie's mother was an excellent seamstress and made clothes for several of the wealthy ladies in the Old Orchard Beach area. Everything Maggie knew about sewing her mother taught her, her unique ability to create beautiful designs was a gift.

Now, living near a big city, Maggie knew that with the right connections she could make a lot of money. Will was always supportive and encouraged her to follow her heart. There was nothing on earth he wouldn't do to make her happy. He bought her the best sewing machine available and allowed her to buy all the fabrics she wanted.

Harriet Johnson had many social connections in town and decided to have a party to welcome her new neighbors. It didn't take Maggie long to become friends with one of the "girls," Carrie Jacobs. Walter and Carrie's father owned the very prominent law firm Jacobs & Johnson LLP in Boston. Before long, the two girls were inseparable.

Maggie spent every day working on new sketches, making patterns, and sewing. Carrie lived in a world that had many social events. After Maggie made Carrie a gown for Carrie's boyfriend's college graduation, some of Carrie's friends wanted Maggie to make dresses for them too. When Carrie got engaged, Maggie said that she would make her friend's wedding dress.

One morning, Maggie woke up feeling sick to her stomach. She immediately became very concerned because Harriet had recently complained about having the same symptons just before Harriett found out she was pregnant. The last thing Maggie wanted was to have a baby now. Word was just starting to get around about how talented she was, and she was finally making money doing what she loved. After a week of being sick, she could no longer hide it from Will, and he insisted that she go to the doctor. Her fear was confirmed. She was due to have a baby around Christmas-time.

Although it took a great deal for Maggie to get used to the idea, Harriet convinced Maggie how much fun they would have raising their children together. The children would be only a month apart in age, and Harriet would be glad to help Maggie out so she could continue working. At the end of November, Harriet gave birth to a son, Donald, and Maggie's Karen was born on Christmas Eve.

Having a daughter changed everything for Maggie. It gave her a whole new focus in her life, and she loved the idea that she could make lots of beautiful outfits for

Karen. It also helped that her friend Carrie was busy taking courses at the local college. Will was deliriously happy. He had married the girl of his dreams, or so he thought, and now he had two girls to dote on.

Maggie's sewing room was transformed into a beautiful nursery. Will built her a folding table that she could use in the kitchen during the day to lay out her patterns and cut her fabrics. Karen was a very happy baby and never gave Maggie any trouble. Karen went on her first train ride when she was six months old, to visit her grandmother in Old Orchard Beach.

The following summer, Maggie's mother suggested that Maggie leave Karen with her for a month or so and come back with Will to get Karen. It took some convincing for Will to agree to this plan, but saying no to Maggie was very difficult. This was the beginning of a tradition, and every summer thereafter, Karen spent time in Maine with her grandmother.

Shortly after Karen turned two, her parents started hearing strange noises during the night. At first they thought it was the wind causing the branches of the bare trees to hit the window and make a scratching sound. Sometimes they would hear squeaking sounds that sounded like they were coming from the floorboards. This was not a nightly occurrence, but the frequency increased as the weeks went on.

Will and Maggie were starting to think that maybe there was something to the story the Johnsons had told them before they bought the house. They both knew it was ludicrous to even entertain such thoughts but decided they needed to get some answers. Shortly after falling asleep that night after their discussion Will woke up and thought he was dreaming. Standing by his bed was Karen, holding her favorite toy, Mr. Chuckles.

After Will had awakened Maggie, they took Karen back to her room and asked her to show them how she had managed to get out of her crib. It was easy for little miss smarty pants to figure out that if she crawled over the side, she could get on the chair next to her crib and climb down. They told Karen they would get her a big girl bed if she would promise to stay in it at night. Karen agreed to stay in her new bed and for almost a year Will and Maggie never heard any unusual sounds during the night.

That summer when she arrived at her grandmother's house, Karen found on her bed a stuffed bear that was almost the same size as she was. Karen named him Mr. Bear and dragged him everywhere she went. When it was time to go home, Karen asked if she could bring Mr. Bear with her, but her parents decided that it would be best to leave him at her grandmother's. Karen agreed, but only if Mr. Bear could sit in her rocking chair until she came back next summer.

In the fall of that year, just before Karen turned three, the night noises started up again. One night, Will got up and found Karen in the living room, sitting in his big green chair and talking to Mr. Chuckles. After putting Karen back to bed, he decided it was time to finish the attic so she could have a larger room. The next morning, Will and Maggie started making plans for making the most of the space upstairs. Both were very excited about making a paradise for their little girl.

3

HER ROOM WAS complete and everything was in its place. Red, white, and blue adorned her sanctuary. Tables, chairs, doll house, curtains, and comforter were in the colors she had asked for. She had shelves for her books and a toy box for her many toys, except for Mr. Chuckles. He was the only one allowed on her bed. Karen didn't care if she never left her beautiful new bedroom, except to go out and play with Donald. The only promise she had to make was not to roam around the house at night.

For as long as Karen could remember, she'd always had to go to bed early. Usually she would fall asleep immediately and wake up long after her parents had gone to sleep. She could stay up for hours making up stories about what went on outside in the dark. She would always tell Mr. Chuckles everything that was going on.

Karen loved to watch the trees dancing when it was windy. The stars looked like Christmas lights, and the moon made everything come alive. In the distance, she could hear the trolley car as it went though town and the Neponset River running downstream. Night was a wonderland of fantasies and the best time to be awake.

On the nights that Karen's parents went out, Ms. Tulloch would come over and stay with her. These were the best nights for Karen. Ms. Tulloch was a very kind old lady who smelled like a freshly opened box of lavender soap. She and her sister Ethel, both retired, lived in the house next door. Ethel would babysit for the Johnsons, and Wilma Tulloch would sit with Karen. Wilma usually sat in the living room in Will's big overstuffed green chair and read a book. The best part was that Ms. Tulloch had very poor hearing so Karen never had to worry about walking around late.

About one month after Karen's fourth birthday, she woke up to the sound of fire engines trucks blowing their horns. They didn't sound like they were very far away. Making her way to the foot of the bed, she very carefully put one foot on the floor at a time. She had perfected the art of never stepping on any of the floorboards that squeaked. The last thing she wanted was to be caught getting up after bedtime.

Even in the dead of winter, Karen was glad she never had to pull down her shades or close her windows. There was no way anyone could see into her room. As she climbed onto the window bench to get a look outside, she started to shiver from the frigid night air coming through the small opening in the window. It was all dark out there. She decided to go back to bed even though it sounded like more sirens were blaring.

Because it was still early, Karen had no trouble falling back to sleep. Later she woke again, but this time, it was to a very loud crunching sound coming from outside her bedroom window. A thick layer of ice covered the new snow that had fallen earlier that evening. As Karen lifted her head from under her thick comforter, the brightness in her room almost blinded her. She had to find out what was going on outside.

The headlights on the car that had just come down their long driveway were still on. The whole front of the house was illuminated like a night game at Fenway Park. She could hardly believe what she was seeing. Two gentlemen in uniforms got out of the car and headed toward the front door of the house.

Very carefully, Karen made her way over to the stairway at the other end of her room. She lay down as close as she could to the first step. She put her ear to the floor. She knew it would be too dangerous to go to the landing because if anyone looked up from the kitchen, they would see her. Unfortunately, at this distance, all she could hear were muffled men's voices coming from the living room.

When she reached the point that she couldn't keep her eyes open any longer, Karen went back to the window for one last check. Someone had turned off the headlights on the car, but now there were lights on in Ms. Tulloch's house. Too tired to care any more, Karen decided to go back to bed.

As soon as she woke the next day, Karen hurried downstairs. For the first time in Karen's life, her mother was not sitting at the kitchen table drinking tea. First, Karen went to the bathroom, getting up on her little stool to brush her teeth and wash her face. Still, no one was up. Rather than going back upstairs, she headed for the living room.

After what seemed like an eternity, Karen's father came out of her parents' room. He told Karen to come and have breakfast. Without another word, he got her cereal and a glass of orange juice. Will took his regular seat at the table next to Karen and asked her if she had slept okay. Karen told him that she heard a lot of noise outside last night and wondered what had happened. Will explained to her that there had been a small fire up in the woods but that it had been put out.

What Karen heard next would haunt her for many years to come. Will, as simply as possible, told his daughter that her mother had gone away for a while. He said that all the clowns at the circus needed new clothes and her mother had had to go to help them. Will told Karen that she needed to be a big girl now and help out when he needed her. Karen's only question was if she could play with Donald later.

After breakfast, Will told Karen to go get dressed and play in her room. He also told her he was not going in to the office and that he would call her when it was time for lunch. An hour later, Karen heard the doorbell ring. It was Harriet Johnson.

Harriet had come over to discuss with Will how best to handle the situation. She thought it would be a good thing if she took Karen to her house for lunch. That way, Karen and Donald could spend the afternoon together, giving Will some time to get things in order. Will agreed and called up to Karen to get her snowsuit on so she could go with Harriet to the Johnsons' house.

As soon as Karen saw Donald, she told him the story about the commotion the night before. The two of them started making up all kinds of stories about what had happened. They both had great imaginations and were never at a loss for creating their own scenario regarding anything. They went on for over an hour, and then Karen told Donald that her mother wasn't home because she had become a circus clown, just like Mr. Chuckles.

When Will went back to work two weeks later, he dropped Karen off at the Johnsons' and picked her up when he got home. This became the new routine in

Karen's life. Every morning, she would pack up some of her things and bring them to Donald's house. Both children were busy with their own projects in the morning. In the afternoon, they were allowed to go outside, weather permitting, and play. Karen had all but moved in with the Johnsons.

4

FROM THE TIME they could walk, Donald and Karen had played together almost every day. It was inevitable that the two children would grow up to be best friends. Now, that Karen's mother was gone, Harriet thought it might be a good idea to have a major distraction for both children. She had always wanted to get a dog, and if they did so now, it would be a positive focus for both children.

In the fall, Donald and Karen would be starting school, and this would keep them busy for the summer months ahead. Walter agreed to get a dog, and as soon as the snow melted, he brought home a boxer puppy. He told the children it was their responsibility to give the puppy a name and to feed and train him. Both children fell in love with the dog immediately.

Donald and Karen spent a long time trying to decide on a name for the new puppy. Karen's first suggestion was to call him Mr. Boxer. Donald told her that she had too many misters already; she had Mr. Bear at her grandmother's house and Mr. Chuckles here. After trying out several names on the new puppy that just didn't work, Karen suggested they name him George. Donald thought it was a great name.

Every day, the children took George for several walks. Life was good. They were having a wonderful time playing with George and watching him get bigger. As the weeks flew by, so did the events of the winter in their minds. Then one morning, Karen realized that she had no way to get to her grandmother's house in June if her mother didn't return soon. Donald told her to ask her father if he would take her.

After their usual quiet dinner that night, Karen asked the question, and her father promised that she would get to see her grandmother in the summer. When June arrived, Ms. Tulloch was the one to take Karen to Maine for her summer vacation. This was the way things went for the next two years, until another of Karen's worlds would come to an end.

When Karen returned from her vacation, she was very surprised how much George had grown. Within a week, she and Donald would be starting school, and both were very concerned what George would do without them. Harriet told the children that she and George would walk with them to and from school, but only for the first few months. After that, they would be on their own.

The children's walk to school was very easy. From Donald's house, they only had to go down one block and turn onto Willow Brook Road and walk one quarter of a mile, and they were at their elementary school. Just before they reached the school, they had to cross over a little wooden bridge. Underneath was a narrow running brook with big trees on either side.

On the way home from school, Karen and Donald would stop and climb on the wooden fence and watch the water flow beneath them. Sometimes they would talk about their day; other times, they would just enjoy the sound of the running brook. Harriet and George would wait on the other side of the bridge, as if they knew it was the children's special time. Once Karen and Donald crossed over the bridge, Harriet would let George run to meet them. The first grade flew by for both children, and when June came around, Karen again went to Maine and came back in time for school.

Karen was doing very well in second grade, and her father was extremely pleased with her report card. Her favorite subjects were penmanship and English. When Karen wasn't reading, she was writing little stories. Whenever she asked, Will would read them. He was always grateful that she never mentioned her mother.

In March, Will got a phone call saying that Karen's grandmother had passed away. He dreaded sharing this news with Karen. He knew how attached she was to her grandmother and was very concerned about how this would affect her. After dinner that evening, he told Karen the news. When she asked what was going to happen to Mr. Bear and how she could bring him home, Will was at a loss for words. There was no way Karen was ever going to see her bear again. There had been a fire and they could not get her grandmother out of the house in time to save her. Everything she'd had was totally destroyed. To the best of his ability, Will told Karen he was truly sorry, her bear was gone forever. There was really nothing he could do about it. Then he told her to only think about the wonderful memories she had with her grandmother.

Karen asked to please be excused from the table so she could go to bed early. Her father excused her. Rather than reading any books that night, Karen crawled into bed with Mr. Chuckles and tried, very, very hard, not to cry. Her father always told her big girls don't cry.

The next day on the way to school, Donald asked several times why Karen was so sad. It took everything Karen had inside her not to cry. She finally told him she would tell him everything at the bridge on the way home. All day,

Donald was concerned about his best friend. As soon as school was over, he grabbed her arm and made her walk as fast as he could to the bridge.

Climbing up on the wooden fence, Karen told Donald that her grandmother had gone to Heaven and now she would never see Mr. Bear again. Donald pulled Karen gently off the fence, looked her right in her eyes, and told her that he would be her Mr. Bear. Then he said he was happy that now they could spend their summers together. Both children left the bridge with smiles on their faces.

That summer, Karen, Donald, and George hung out together. They took long walks and played ball. Sometimes, Harriet would make them a picnic lunch to take to the park. When they went to the ice cream parlor, Donald always went inside and got the ice cream. Then they would sit at one of the little tables outside, under the awning, and share their treat with George.

5

THIRD AND FOURTH grades went by without any major problems or catastrophes for Karen. The more time Karen and Donald were together, the more they discussed the future. Donald knew he wanted to go to Harvard and become a lawyer like his dad. Karen wanted to write books, but first, she wanted to be a mother. They talked, many times, about how lucky they were to have each other and about how when they got married, they would have four children, no more, no less.

One Friday night in mid-August, Karen's father told her they needed to talk about something very serious. After he finished the dishes, he told Karen to meet him in the living room. He took his green chair, and she sat in one of the high-backed chairs across the room.

Will began by saying that he had made some very important decisions regarding their life together. He said he had taken a few weeks off from work because he was very tired and needed to rest. Then he dropped the bomb.

"Karen, I want you to know how very proud I am of you. You are an excellent student in school and you are becoming a fine young lady. Next month you will be entering fifth grade and in December you will turn ten. It is time for you to be around other females. You need to learn many things about yourself that I cannot teach you.

"After very careful consideration, I have decided that you will be going to a home for girls, located about one hour from here. It was not easy to get you in there, but Mr. Johnson wrote a lovely letter of recommendation and they agreed to accept you.

"You will stay there until you graduate from high school. It is a fine institution, and you will receive a good education. They have visiting days every other month when I can come and spend time with you. In the meantime, we can write letters.

"You have the weekend to get your things in order and pack a few of your clothes. You can bring all your writing materials and a few books. Everything else will be provided for you when you get there. I will drive you to the home on Monday morning."

Karen asked if she could please be excused. She needed to go to the bathroom because she felt sick. Will was a bit puzzled. Karen had never complained about being sick. Before excusing her, he told her that if she had any questions, they could talk about them in the morning. With that said, he got up and went directly to his room. Once inside, he closed the door.

This was the first time Karen had ever thrown up. As soon as she felt better, she called Donald to tell him that she was sick and would see him in the morning. When he asked about their nightly walk with George, she told him to go by himself. Once Karen made it up to her room, she put on her pajamas, held Mr. Chuckles, and cried until she fell asleep. She really didn't care that she was "not a big girl" any more.

After Donald hung up the phone, he went to his mother and told her the story. Because Harriet was privy to Will's plans, she thought it was best to tell Donald what was happening. When Will asked if he could go with Karen on Monday, Harriet told him no. She did, however, promise that he could go with his father and Mr. Peterson on visiting days. She also told Donald that he and Karen could write to each other, as often as they wanted. It was a long night for both children.

On Saturday morning, Karen woke up very early and very hungry. Her eyes hurt and were difficult to open. Then she remembered what had happened the night before. Looking in the mirror, she was horrified at what she saw. *So this is why big girls don't cry,* she thought. *Next day, you really look ugly.*

After breakfast, she went to see Donald. George sensed that something was wrong and jumped up on Karen when she walked in the door. As soon as Karen sat down at the kitchen table, George laid down on the floor next to her. The two children discussed the situation for a long time and came up with a plan. Every Saturday, they would write a letter and tell each other everything about their week. With that settled, they took the picnic lunch that Harriet had made for them, and Karen, Donald and George left for the park.

6

CLOSING HER SUITCASE, Karen took one last look around her room to make sure she had everything she needed. She and Donald had said everything they had to say the night before. He had given her a big hug and her first kiss, on the cheek. Karen had even let George kiss her face, although it normally wasn't allowed. Karen would miss them all, but in her heart, she knew her father had made the right decision. Before leaving, she walked over to Mr. Chuckles for one last hug. He always made her smile.

Karen and her father rode in silence, each engrossed in private thoughts. When they approached the entrance to the school, Karen was pleasantly surprised. The Wesley Home was a large two-story white building set back from the road and surrounded by 20 acres of tall trees.

The owner of the property had built the structure for the sole purpose of providing a loving and caring home for girls in need. When he had passed away, he had left suffi-cient funds in his estate to run the institution for many years. In addition, donations from several churches throughout the state and from local organizations and town merchants provide additional support to the facility.

Inside the front door, Karen and her father were greeted by Ms. Fletcher, the headmistress. Ms. Fletcher invited them into the visitor's center to complete the final paperwork. When they were finished, Will thanked the headmistress, and then said good-bye to Karen. He told her he would write to her later in the week and that if she needed anything, she should let Ms. Fletcher know and she would contact him.

Karen's first stop was the dining room, where lunch was being served. There were five tables, each with four chairs. At each setting was a nameplate. There was one long table for the staff. Mrs. Fletcher explained that every day the nameplates were moved around to different tables and chairs. This taught the girls to socialize with each other in a relaxed environment. Karen thought it was a very nice way for them to get to know each other and for everyone to feel equal.

After lunch Ms. Watson, one of the three workers, came over to Karen to introduce herself. She would escort Karen around the facility and familiarize her with how things were done. She explained that the school could house up to 20 girls, but at the present time they had only 13 ranging in age from three to seven making Karen the oldest. Upstairs was one dormitory for the younger girls and five single bedrooms for the older ones. Bathrooms, showers, and a large dressing room separated the two sleeping quarters.

When they reached Karen's room, Ms. Watson told her she was the only girl, at this time, in a private room. All of the other children were too young. Karen's room had a single bed, a dresser, a desk, and a small closet. No curtains were needed on the windows because they were on the second floor. The room was nothing like Karen's beautiful red, white, and blue bedroom at home, but then again, nothing was like it was before.

On the desk was a schedule of the activities for the week, the times meals were served, and a list of chores she would be responsible for. Karen would be expected to help out with the younger girls in any way she could. This was good news for Karen, because she would have someone to read to and play games with.

The following Friday evening when she entered the dining room, Karen saw two letters alongside her plate. One was from Donald and the other from her father. When she arrived back to her room, she put them on her table. She wanted to save them until it was time for her quiet hour before going to bed.

The next few weeks went quickly, and Karen was making the best of her new life. When school started, she was ready for the change. The children attended a private girl's school located only a few blocks from Wesley.

The first two years went by quickly, and Karen saw her father, Donald, and Donald's parents every other month. The letters from her father and Donald came regularly once a week and she returned one to each. When both Karen and Donald were in their first year of junior high school, they found school more interesting than before. They had always been straight-A students and had breezed through elementary school.

Donald was enrolled in a private prep school for grades 7 through 12. This was where he met his new best friend, Oliver. Both of the boys shared the same goals, each wanting to go to Harvard and to become a lawyer. Karen was glad that Donald had someone to hang out with. She was very busy helping the younger girls with their studies, teaching them to read and write.

Life was going well, and Karen had a sense of peace in her world, until a month after she started 10th grade. Karen awoke one morning in the most excruciating pain imaginable. She could not get out of bed and lay there until someone realized she was missing from the breakfast table. Ms. Watson was the one to find her lying in bed and sobbing. An ambulance was called, and Karen was admitted to the hospital.

The doctors discovered that Karen had a cyst on the tip of her tailbone. This particular type of cyst had formed before her birth. If bacteria had not caused it to become infected, it would never have been a problem. Now, however, it was extremely infected and surgery could not be performed until the infection was cleared up.

Karen was given antibiotics and pain medication intravenously. The doctors suggested that her father wait until the surgery was scheduled before coming to see her. The following week, surgery was performed and the cyst was removed. Only Will and Walter were at the hospital when Karen came out of the recovery room. Under major protest, Donald had remained in school and sent her a beautiful card and flowers.

Coming out of the anesthesia, Karen felt like she was floating somewhere in space. She was lying on her left side with a bumper pillow along her back so she could not roll over and lie flat. Her first thought was that she must have died. The only time she had ever been sick was when she and Donald had had the measles. She had never experienced anything like this before, and all she could remember was the pain. Fear overtook her, and she started to cry. Will immediately called the nurse.

After receiving additional pain medication, Karen was once again calm. It was then that she saw her father and Walter, for only a minute, and went back to sleep. Later that night after being reassured that Karen was doing well, Will and Walter went home. The next morning when the doctor came to check on Karen, he became a bit concerned. When he tapped her knee with his little rubber hammer, Karen made no response.

After checking the dressing on Karen's wound, the doctor decided to consult one of his colleagues. They both agreed to wait a day or so and see how Karen progressed. Days turned into a week, and although the wounds from her surgery were healing, Karen still had no feeling from the waist down. She had to be lifted out of bed to take sitz baths. Karen could not stand up without help. Several other doctors were called in on her case.

Feeling very alone and scared that she would never be able to walk again, Karen started withdrawing into her own world, further and further. Her father came to visit once a week and even brought Donald and Harriet along to see if that would help improve Karen's mental state. Nothing was working. Every day, Karen asked the same question, over and over again: "Why can't I move my legs?"

It was the youngest intern on the team, a Dr. Glassman, who finally stepped forward with a bold and unconventional explanation for what he felt the problem was. All the members on staff agreed that it was worth looking into. They had nothing to lose at this point and called Will to the hospital for a meeting. They did not want to give him this news over the phone.

Just two months before Karen was hospitalized, Will sold his car because he wasn't comfortable driving any more. Now, Walter took him everywhere. When the two men arrived at the hospital, Will asked Walter to please attend the meeting with him. The doctors told Will and Walter that they believed fear was causing Karen's paralysis—a fear so strong that the pain would return, so that Karen's brain would not allow her to move.

Karen's father spoke first. "Let me have some time with her alone. If this is truly the problem, I think I can help fix it." Walter said that he would wait in the cafeteria and when Will was ready to leave, they could meet there.

Karen was awake when Will entered her room. He pulled the visitor chair close to her bed and took her hand.

He told her that the doctors had completed every test possible and all agreed that her surgery was very successful. He also explained the doctors' belief for that the reason Karen couldn't walk or move her legs. Will went on to say that Karen could do whatever she wanted if she put her mind to it. He told her that today was the day she would get out of bed and get on with her life. Karen just looked at her father in disbelief. He had never been so harsh with her before. Will continued by saying that the doctors had removed the cyst and there was nothing inside that could hurt her.

There was always a tiny bit of fear inside Karen when her father spoke to her with his stern voice. When he put out his hands and took hers in his, she grabbed hold. Very carefully, Will pulled her into a sitting position, then took her legs very slowly and turned her body around so she was sitting on the edge of the bed. "Now you are going to stand up and take one step at a time," he said.

As she slid down off the bed and let her feet touch the floor, Karen began to shake. "Oh Daddy, I'm standing, I can do it, I can do it."

Will looked at this little girl, so tall and thin, and said in a soft tone, "I knew you could do it." After helping her to the guest chair, Will left the room. Outside her room three of the doctors were waiting for him. All Will said was, "She is sitting in the chair, and she will be fine."

Five days later, Karen was released from the hospital. After two months of therapy, she was feeling more like herself. By the time January came, she had made up all her classes and was back in school. When she started her senior year in high school, the previous year was barely a memory.

Donald came with his parents and Will to Karen's graduation, and there was a small reception at Wesley in her honor. Karen noticed that her father had been losing weight over the past few months. He told her that it was nothing and that he would try and eat more. She had made a decision to stay on at Wesley for another six months to attend a business school in town. Classes started on July 1, and she would be home before Christmas.

SAYING GOOD-BYE

Deadly Affair
Best Man
Decisions

7

RETURNING HOME IN mid-December, Karen was a bit taken aback by her father's condition. The very first thing she did was go up to her bedroom and look around. So many years ago, it had seemed so much bigger. Everything was in the exact place she had left it; it would always be her sanctuary.

After putting her things away, Karen went to see Harriet and Walter. They told her that her father had not been able to work for many years. They had wanted to tell her, but he had made them promise not to. They had honored his decision.

For Christmas that year, Donald gave Karen an engagement ring that had belonged to his grandmother. Although his parents thought it would be best to wait a few years before Donald and Karen married, Donald said they would be married in June. Karen's father had given them his blessing without much resistance.

Already halfway through his first year at Harvard, Donald was doing very well at school. His best friend, Oliver, had received a scholarship to attend the University of California and eventually would attend UC Law School. Oliver had taken his mother with him to California. Both boys knew they would always stay in touch. They had become very close friends over the past six years, and Oliver would be Donald's best man when he and Karen wed.

In early January, Karen accepted a position as the secretary to the editor of the local newspaper. It was only a short walk to work, and she was glad to be close in case her father needed her. Three months before Karen's wedding, her father took a turn for the worse. He told her that he must put his affairs in order.

One night in late March, Karen went to his room and sat with her father, as he had requested. Will asked her to go into his closet and get a gray tin box buried in the back, behind his shoes. He said the key was in his desk drawer. He told Karen that the most important thing to remember in life is that hate is a poison and it will kill you. His last words were, "Karen, remember that I have always loved you and I am very proud of the young lady you have become."

"I love you too, Daddy," Karen replied. Karen kissed him on the cheek and took the box up to her room. After getting ready for bed, she rearranged her pillows and made herself comfortable. Inside the box, Karen found Will's bank book and a copy of his last will and testament. In the bottom of the box, she found three envelopes and a note that read, "Please read these notes in order."

The first letter her father had written told her that he had a sister named Ann. When Ann was 17 years old, she had found out she was pregnant and run off to New York with her boyfriend. Ann had given birth to a girl she named Barbara, but Ann and her boyfriend had never married. Barbara now lived in Queens with her husband, Len. They would very much like to get to know Karen and hoped that she would contact them. At the bottom of the note was Barbara's address and phone number.

The second letter explained how Karen's grandmother had died. In the envelope was a savings account book with one deposit in the amount of $22,200 that Will had received from her insurance company after the fire. The letter went on to say

> *I bought this house from Walter Johnson when your mother and I got married. He owned both the houses. When I sent you to Wesley, I never went back to work. I could no longer function in the outside world and fell into a very deep depression. I tried very hard not to let you see it when I visited you.*

> *When my money ran out, I made a deal with Walter, and he bought the house back from me. Each month, I paid him a small amount of rent. There will be a small pension from the government due to my many years of service in the Army. Other than that, I don't have much to leave you because my medical bills ate most of my savings.*

> *Walter did promise me that he would give the house to you and Donald as a wedding present. Please save your grandmother's money for an emergency.*

The third letter began by telling Karen how her parents had met and how much they both loved her, then it continued

> *Now, I need to tell you about your mother. I was ashamed to share this story with you all these years, but you have a right to know the truth. To the best of my memory, here are the facts.*

> *Your mother had a close friend named Carrie Jacobs. Carrie is the daughter of Walter's partner*

in his law firm, Jacobs & Johnson LLD. She was getting married in April the year your mother left us. Your mother was making her wedding dress. First your mother designed the dress and, after making whatever changes Carrie wanted, started putting it together. The day of the accident, your mother told me that she had to take some more measurements on Carrie. She said she would be home by dinnertime.

I purposely came home early from work so she could leave to go to Carrie's. When your mother didn't come home for dinner, I called the Jacobs' home to see what had happened to her. There was no answer. I called a few more times and was still not able to get anyone home.

Just after you went up to bed, Walter came over to tell me that there had been an accident. Walter had just received a phone call from Mr. Jacobs, his law firm partner and dear friend. He thought it would be best to have Walter deliver the news in person, rather than having someone phone me. From what I understood, Mr. & Mrs. Jacobs had taken Carrie away for a few days. Carrie's older brother Mark did not go with them. They were scheduled to return home the following day but decided to come back early that night.

The night of the accident happened, it was bitter cold. When the Jacobs arrived home around 8 o'clock, they saw lights on in the garage. From outside they could hear Mike's car running. After opening the door to the garage, they found the bodies of your mother and Mark in the backseat of his car.

The fire department was dispersed, along with the paramedics, etc., and that was why you heard all the sirens that night. There was no fire in the hills. Later, the police came and took me to the morgue to identify your mother's body. Ms. Tulloch came over to stay with you when I left.

The coroner said it was apparent that they had turned on the car heater to try and stay warm and had died of carbon monoxide poisoning. I had your mother cremated and sent her ashes to your grandmother. Later, Carrie admitted she knew that your mother and Mark had been carrying on an affair for months.

The morning after the accident, I made up the story about your mother going to work in the circus. I came up with the idea because of your attachment to Mr. Chuckles. You carried that red, white, & blue cloth clown with the beautiful porcelain face, hands, and feet around with you everywhere. You talked to him nonstop, especially at night. I thought that this was the easiest way for you to understand why she was gone.

Over the years, I lost sight of you, my precious daughter. All I saw was the young wife that I once loved so dearly. I truly regret that I became so cold and what seemed like unfeeling. I especially regret how hard I was on you when you were in the hospital.

Please, Karen, forgive me. I truly loved you more than you will ever know.

Daddy

Until the early morning hours finally brought a glimpse of dawn to the sky, Karen sat in her bed reading, and rereading, her father's letters. Now she knew what had happened to the warm and loving father she had so adored as a small child. This wonderful man had been taken from her by her mother many years ago.

When daylight came, Karen went downstairs to find that during the night, Will had been reunited with his beloved Maggie. Later that day, Karen handed Donald the letter explaining her mother's accident and asked him to destroy it after he read it. They never discussed the contents of the letter. A small memorial service was held at the Johnsons', which enabled Karen to put the past behind her, at least for a while.

8

.

THE LAST OF their new furniture was scheduled to be delivered today. Everything had a fresh coat of paint, and 29 Crabtree Lane had never looked better. The master bedroom was complete with new drapes, matching comforter, and several throw pillows. Karen had bought a new kitchen set and redecorated the living room. She had even replaced her father's overstuffed green chair. She wanted a fresh start.

Karen converted the second bedroom into an office for her and Donald. Donald needed a place to study, and she needed to write. Since she had gone to live at Wesley, Karen had had very little time to spend writing entries in her journals. The only room that she didn't change, except to paint the walls, was her bedroom. It would always be her private space, until they had their own children, and that was fine with Donald.

It was wonderful for Karen to have Barbara's help after her father passed away. Within a few days after they talked for the first time, Barbara had driven down from New York and spent two weeks. Karen remembered how shocked she was when Barbara stepped out of her car. Looking at her was like seeing herself in 15 years. They had so many of the same features that they could pass for sisters. The biggest difference in the two women was that

Barbara had short curly hair and Karen's was long and straight as a pin.

While she was in town, Barbara found a dress for the wedding. When Karen asked Barbara to be her matron of honor, she was elated. During one of Barbara's phone calls to Len, he offered to give Karen away, but she told him no. She explained that Walter had been like a second father to her all these years and she didn't want to hurt him. Len, of course, understood.

All that was left now was one more fitting of Karen's dress. Knowing that she and Donald would finally be getting married was overwhelming. They had talked so much about it for so many years that it had seemed like it would never happen. Walter and Harriet were going to transfer the deed to the house over to Donald and Karen, as they had promised Will. Barbara and Len gave them a week in Cape Cod for their honeymoon, but Donald kept all the details as a surprise for Karen.

Oliver was scheduled to arrive the afternoon of the rehearsal. For the few days he would be in town, he would be staying at the Johnsons' home. Harriet had also offered to have Barbara and Len stay with them, but they had already made reservations at a lovely local B&B. Walter booked a chapel for the service; the reception would be at the Johnsons' home.

On the morning of the rehearsal, Karen needed to go downtown to pick up a few last-minute things. While she was out shopping, she thought maybe she would try on a few lipsticks. Harriet had very tactfully suggested that she might like using a little lip color, at least for the wedding. Karen had never worn makeup of any kind. After spending a few minutes at the makeup counter, she decided that Vaseline was about as daring as she could get. She never worried about her hair because if it wasn't in a ponytail, it was twirled up in a knot on top of her head.

Barbara and Len were waiting for Karen when she arrived home. They were taking her to the chapel later and wanted to spend some time with her alone first. Len was very easygoing, and he and Karen hit it off immediately. It was nice for all of them to have some kind of family again, and they all looked forward to spending holidays together.

Arriving at the chapel, Karen noticed that Donald's car was already there. Walking into the vestibule, she saw him talking to the clergyman. Beside Donald was a man she had never seen before. He was about her height, 5'8", and had short brown hair. Nothing about him seemed unusual; he was just an average-looking guy about Donald's age. Karen turned to Barbara and said, "I think that must be Oliver, Donald's best man."

When Donald motioned to Karen to come over, Karen asked Barbara and Len to come with her. After giving her a kiss on the cheek, Donald said, "Karen, this is my friend Oliver." As Karen turned to look at Oliver, their eyes locked and she extended her hand. He took her hand in both of his and said, "Karen, what a pleasure to finally meet you. I feel like I've known you forever. Donald has told me so much about you, except how beautiful you are."

Speechless, barely able to bring a smile to her face, Karen felt warmth penetrate through places in her body she had never known existed. Finally, grasping reality, she could only say, "Nice to meet you too, Oliver." Things after that got a bit fuzzy. She was petrified to look at Oliver again. All she kept thinking was that she had to stay far away from him until she could figure out what had just happened.

The rehearsal didn't take very long, as they had chosen to use the standard version of the wedding vows. Harriet had invited everyone to the house for dinner, and Karen told Donald that she needed to stop by her house first. Barbara was a bit concerned, and as soon as they got inside, she asked Karen what had happened. She said that she thought Karen looked a bit pale.

Trying hard not to reveal what she had felt when she had met Oliver, Karen said she just needed to take an aspirin before going over to Donald's. Although Barbara suspected it was more than that, she didn't press the issue. She knew that they would have time to talk about it later. When Karen finally got into the bathroom and closed the door, she looked into the mirror. All she could see was Oliver looking back at her. Gently tapping her cheeks and shaking her head, she said, half out loud, "Snap out of it."

As soon as Karen saw the seating arrangements at the table, she felt more relaxed. Harriet was on one end and Walter on the other. On one side of the table were Barbara and Len, and on the other side, Donald, Karen, and Oliver. Although she would have liked to change seats with Donald, at least she wouldn't have to look directly at Oliver while they were eating. During the dinner, she was able to carry on a civil conversation with Oliver, always cautious not to look at him directly. He didn't make it easy; even the tone of his voice was warm, and, once or twice, their elbows touched, sending flashes of heat through her body.

Len went back to the B&B by himself and let the girls spend the night alone. He would pick them up in the morning and take them to the chapel for the eleven o'clock ceremony. Everyone was invited back to the Johnsons' for a catered buffet lunch afterward. Donald wanted to make sure that they were able to leave in time to arrive at Cape Cod by evening.

As soon as Len pulled out of the driveway, Barbara said that they should have a glass of wine and talk about this Oliver Ryan guy. Half hoping that Barbara would bring it up, half hoping that she wouldn't, Karen got two glasses, and they went into the living room.

Barbara started right in. "Okay, Karen, what's up with Oliver? A blind person could see the immediate chemistry between you two. If you weren't getting married tomorrow, Oliver would have you married to him in a heartbeat. I just can't believe that Donald was totally oblivious to Oliver's reaction to you. You know, Karen, I do believe that there is such a thing as love at first sight."

Karen just sat there, looking into space as Barbara carried on about her feelings. Even though Karen thought what Barbara was saying was a bunch of nonsense, she had to admit that it had been the strangest evening of her life. She really didn't know what to make of any of it. Every time she closed her eyes, all she could see was Oliver. Finally, Karen said, "Oh, come on, Barbara, I truly believe you are making a mountain out of a molehill. Let's just go to bed."

The day Karen had waited so many years for had finally arrived. Looking like a princess, veil covering her face, she stood with her arm in Walter's at the entrance to the chapel. As the organist started playing "The Wedding March," Karen repeated one prayer over and over again in her head: *Please, God, let me say, 'I take thee, Donald.'*

9

MARRIED LIFE WAS just about what Karen had thought it should be. Donald was a sweet and loving husband. She really couldn't ask for anything more. Harriet taught Karen how to cook some basic meals. On special occasions, Karen and Donald would treat themselves and go out to dinner. Sundays were always spent at the Johnsons'.

The holidays had a whole new meaning for Karen now. She and Donald had worked out a plan that every Thanksgiving, Karen and Donald would go to New York and spent it with Barbara and Len. Because Barbara and Len owned a travel agency in Manhattan, they always found good airfare for them. Len would pick them up at LaGuardia and treated them to a wonderful weekend in the city. Christmas was at Harriet and Walter's. Barbara and Len would arrive on December 23 so they could celebrate Karen's birthday starting with a birthday brunch Christmas Eve morning.

When Donald graduated from Harvard, Harriet threw a big party for him. Barbara and Len came down for the event. Knowing that Oliver was also graduating, Harriet thought it would be nice if they could celebrate together. Oliver said he would like nothing better than to fly out and join in on the festivities but he couldn't. His mother was not feeling well and he didn't feel that he should leave her alone in California.

Both boys entered law school in the fall, Donald at Harvard Law and Oliver at UC Law. Although they had not seen each other since the wedding, they spoke on the phone about once a month. Oliver always told Donald to please give Karen his love. Karen said the same thing every time: "That's nice."

In his second year of law school, Donald told Karen that he thought it was time to start trying to having a family. He was already working at the firm with his father and knew that someday he would be a partner. Karen was still working for the newspaper but had been transferred into the editing department. She really liked what she was doing but, more importantly, had been waiting years to become a mother.

It wasn't until Donald was halfway through his last year of law school that they started getting concerned that Karen wasn't pregnant. They agreed to wait until he graduated before consulting with a specialist. June came and went, and all that was left was for Donald to pass the bar exam. In August, they decided to drive up to Old Orchard Beach for a few days before the Labor Day weekend.

In mid-September, they finally agreed to find out if there was a medical reason for Karen's inability to become pregnant. Within a week, all the results were in and they had their answer. Yes, there was a good reason. Because of the possibility that Karen's mother had taken a certain drug, Karen would never be able to conceive. At this point, she felt her life was over. All she had ever wanted was to give Donald children and be a good mother. This was the most devastating news of her life.

Choosing not to discuss their situation, they both went on with their daily lives. It was Karen who eventually broke the silence. One Friday night in early October,

Karen announced that she had quit her job. She said she was going to New York to spend a few weeks with Barbara. She needed to get away and think about their future. Donald tried to convince her not to go, but once her mind was set there was no changing it, and he knew it.

The following morning, Karen packed her VW bug with a few of her things and started to leave. As she pulled out of the driveway, she stopped. Donald was still on the porch, tears in his eyes, hoping that she had changed her mind. When she approached him, all she said was, "I forgot Mr. Chuckles. I'll call you later." By the time she got to the highway, everything hit her. Pulling every ounce of courage within her, she just kept taking deep breaths and telling herself that she'd figure it all out later. Right now she was on her first adventure by herself.

The guest room where she and Donald slept on their visits was ready when Karen arrived. Sandy and Candy, Barbara and Len's two cocker spaniels, greeted her with their usual excitement. Karen loved them and knew they would be good therapy for her. She could give them all the loved she wanted, knowing they would never hurt her, just love her back. This was how she would heal, if that was even possible.

Donald called every evening for the first week, but Karen couldn't bring herself to talk with him. She spent most of her days in her room, trying to write, but nothing was making sense. She took the dogs for a walk twice a day and let them hang out on her bed whenever they wanted. All she kept thinking was that she should go away and be alone, forever.

Barbara and Len were very supportive and told her she could stay as long as she wanted. On Sunday, Karen called Donald and told him she needed more than another week. She agreed that they needed to talk, but she wasn't ready. There were many things to consider. It was her fault that

Donald would never become a father. Karen and Barbara finally sat down, and Karen let it all out. There really was no question as to what needed to be done; it was just how and when.

The night before Thanksgiving, Donald arrived. At first things were a little uncomfortable, but the two pups had a way of providing a warm distraction. They were only four years old and still very playful. Thanksgiving dinner was the usual group: Barbara and Len's best friends, Karen and Donald. Everything was festive, and they all took their usual stroll through Manhattan after dinner.

On Friday morning, Donald borrowed Len's car so he and Karen could take a ride out to Jones Beach. They needed to be by the water and work things out. Barbara gave them a large thermos full of hot chocolate and a bag of cookies. Len put a couple of towels and two old army blankets in the car. Even though the sun was shining brightly, it was a typical fall day, the air crisp. Traffic was light heading east on the Long Island Expressway and even lighter when they reached the Northern State Parkway. While everyone else in the world was out shopping for Christmas bargains, Donald and Karen were out to decide their future.

The parking lot was deserted with the exception of three cars. A few people were walking on the beach with dogs, and the tide had just started going out. After putting the blankets down on the sand, Donald and Karen took off their shoes and socks and rolled up their pants legs. It was a tradition with them. No matter what beach they went to or what time of year it was, they always put their feet in the salty water.

The frigid water broke the silence that had surrounded them since they had left Queens. "I will always love you," Donald said.

Karen replied, "I will always love you too, Mr. Bear." Hysterical crying followed their embrace.

Back on the blanket, they wrapped themselves up tightly. For a long time they just stared at the sea of blue in total silence. Knowing that their life together was coming to an end, they clung to each other, two hearts totally broken, wondering if they would ever mend. He had been her lifeline for as many years as she could remember, and Karen was his life.

On the ride back, they talked about their special chat sessions at the bridge on Willow Brook Road and of their fun times with George. A long time ago, Harriet had told them both the story of 29 Crabtree Lane and Old Man Fitzgerald. Today they wondered if maybe there was some kind of curse on the house after all. Donald said that he would move back into his parents' house and they could sell, or burn it down if they wanted to. He would never stay in that house again.

It was almost dark by the time they got back to Barbara and Len's. Traffic was bumper to bumper and they were both starving. All they had that day was the hot chocolate and cookies that Barbara had given them. Everyone agreed that they should keep their original plans and go to their favorite Italian restaurant in Manhattan for dinner. It was the place they always went on the day after Thanksgiving.

Donald changed his flight so he could fly back to Boston the next day. Early Saturday morning, after he packed his bag, Karen and Donald had coffee and scones in silence. He then said his good-byes to his dear friends and turned to Karen for one last hug. There were no more tears to be shed. When Len said that he was going down to get the car, Donald started to follow.

"Wait, wait, I have something for you!" Karen yelled. When she came back, she handed Donald Mr. Chuckles.

"He always made me smile. Maybe he can do the same for you." It was time to let the past go; it was time for her to stand on her own, without any crutches.

10

IN DECEMBER, BARBARA told Karen that she and Len had made plans for the holidays. One of their friends in the travel business had a lovely inn in Vermont, and Barbara booked two rooms for them, including the dogs. Barbara thought the holidays this year should be spent someplace far away from everyone and everything familiar to them. They would be leaving on December 23 and would come back on New Year's Day.

The first snow of the season had fallen a few days before they left. The roads were clear and the scenery was beautiful. When they arrived in the small rural town, Karen started to feel a bit of excitement. She knew something about this was going to be very good for her. As much as she loved the beach, she felt more at home in the woods, surrounded by big old trees. The woods reminded her of her grandmother's and some of her best childhood memories.

From the entrance to the inn, they could smell bread baking in the kitchen. Karen's room was small and cozy, and everything was beautifully decorated for the holidays. She couldn't bring herself to send any Christmas cards and at this point did not know if she ever would again. She did, however, love where they were staying. The day before she left, she received a birthday card from Donald, signed, "Love Always, Mr. Bear."

On their dining room table the next morning was a beautiful bouquet of flowers and a birthday card for Karen from Barbara and Len. Later, Karen and Barbara left Len with the dogs and went into town to look through the shops. They stopped in a candle store and bought some hand-dipped pine-scented candles to take back with them. That night, they sat by the big fireplace and listened to Christmas carols while drinking some brandy before turning in early.

On the day after Christmas, Karen was glancing through the local newspaper and stopped on the "homes for sale" section. There was a picture of a few newly built cabins located about a mile away from the inn. She asked Barbara if they could take a ride and look at them. Len volunteered to take her. He knew Barbara was a good driver, but, being unfamiliar with the area, he felt more comfortable driving them himself. Both Barbara and Len were happy that Karen was beginning to show an interest in something again.

When they got to the area where the cabins were, the first thing Karen saw was an A-framed log cabin. A large deck stretched across the entire front of the cabin. When they walked inside, they were surprised to see that the entire cabin was one big room with areas sort of separated. On the right side was the family room with a kitchen/dining area behind it. On the left side was a bedroom, bath and a small laundry room. Separating the two spaces was a floor-to-ceiling fireplace open on both sides. It reminded Karen of her bedroom in the attic. This would become Karen's new dream. The A-frame was absolutely the perfect place to live her life and write.

As soon as Karen, Barbara, and Len arrived back in Queens, Karen decided to start working on her first book.

All she had to do was to figure out how she would support herself. The money she had received from her grandmother was not to be used unless she was in dire straits. The large deposit Donald's father had made to her account when they got divorced was only to be used to buy a house. There was still money left from her father's bank account, but she knew she must be very frugal.

For the time being, she could stay where she was and concentrate on her writing. By living with Barbara and Len, she was helping her cousins out financially. They were able to cancel the dog walker, their once-a-week cleaning lady, and the cost of boarding their dogs when they traveled. Karen was also becoming a very good cook. She now took care of all the food shopping, dry-cleaning errands, and any other task that would help them out. With the exception of Saturday night when they all went out to dinner, she was cooking all their meals.

The months seemed to pass quickly. In June, Karen's divorce was final and she changed her name back to Peterson. In July, Barbara told her that she and Len would be leaving that weekend on a business trip. They were going to New Hampshire to check out an inn that they were thinking of adding to their list. Karen never gave it much thought because they often took trips pertaining to their business.

On Sunday evening when Barbara and Len arrived home, they told Karen that they had made a decision and wanted to speak to her about their plans. While in New Hampshire, they had found a very large old farmhouse that was for sale and had put a deposit on it. The week before, someone had made them an offer to buy their agency in Manhattan. When they saw this place, they had known it was a sign for them to get out of New York. They had always wanted to have a B&B of their own, and this was the place to have it.

They had no concerns about selling their condo because there was a buyer's waiting list. A three-bedroom place in their neighborhood was a premium. All they needed to know now was if Karen would have any interest in coming with them. Because she was so intrigued with the A-frame, they thought she might want to join them in their new adventure.

Karen told Barbara she needed time to sort this all out. She did say that she would give them an answer within a few days. The biggest issue for Karen was deciding exactly what she really wanted to do with her life. Of course, she wanted to write books, but that wasn't something she would ever count on as her financial support. Karen really needed a plan for now and for the future. Subconsciously, she was happy that she was being forced to take some action.

That week, Karen began looking through the various want ads to get an idea of what positions were available in the outside world. She knew that she was an excellent stenographer and should have no problem getting an office job; however, there was still the issue that she wanted to be a mother more than anything. She felt that if she could care for a child, it might help her work through the pain of not being able to have a child of her own.

Domestic positions were plentiful enough, but finding the right one might not be easy. After circling several ads for positions in the Queens area, Karen started looking in the Long Island section. One particular ad caught her attention: "Lost Wife. Need live-in woman to care for two girls. Room, board, meals included, salary negotiable. Call evenings after 6 PM." Later than evening, she called and spoke to a Louie Piazzola.

WHERE TO HIDE

The Nanny
The Red Rooster
The Photographer

11

IN HER CONVERSATION with Louie Piazzola,
Karen set up a meeting for the following Saturday afternoon. Louie was to come to Queens at two o'clock in the
afternoon to interview Karen. He explained that he felt it
was best to screen applicants in their own surroundings
before letting them come to his home. Karen thought this
was a very professional way to handle the situation and
also showed that Louie was protective of his children.

When she answered the door, Karen was surprised at
the size of him. Louie was a rather large, rugged-looking
man. He said that he was a welder for a construction firm
on Long Island. He had two daughters; Jenny was eight
years old, and Melissa had just turned six. The previous
year, his wife had left him and the girls for some punk she
had met in a bar. Eventually, his wife and her boyfriend
had moved to Florida. Before she left, his wife had signed
the divorce papers and given up custody of her children.
Karen felt sick to her stomach after hearing this story.

Louie wanted to know all about Karen and why she
would want this position. As briefly as possible, she gave
him the facts. The only thing she mentioned about her
mother was that she had died when Karen was very young.
When she asked who had been taking care of the girls for

the past year, Louie said that his sister was living with him but was getting married the next month.

Karen and Louie made plans for Karen to drive out to Long Island the next day to meet the girls. If everything went well, she could have the position. That night, Barbara, Len, and Karen went to their usual spot for a few drinks and dinner. She told them the story of her visitor. Len was a little concerned at first that Louie might not be on the up and up.

Although Karen did not have much experience in dealing with the outside world, in many ways, she was wise beyond her years. Louie had given her two letters of recommendation, one from his family physician, one from his local priest. Both letters confirmed his story. Barbara and Len gave their full support. Their only regret was that she would not be going to New Hampshire with them.

The next day, Karen drove to Long Island. The Piazzola home was a four-bedroom colonial with a large, very well manicured front lawn. Before parking the car, Karen double-checked the street number. Satisfied that this was the right place, she parked on the street and walked up to the front door. Much to her surprise, the inside of the house was very tastefully furnished with all oak furniture. Louie invited her into the living room and told her he would call the girls.

The sight of two lovely girls coming down the stairs stirred up many emotions in Karen, none of them familiar to her. Each of the girls introduced herself and took a seat on the couch. Louie explained that Karen would like to spend some time with them that day to get to know them and that Karen was considering coming to live with them when their Aunt Loretta got married. Then he asked the girls if they would like to show Karen around the house. Jenny was the first one to pipe up, "Sure, Daddy, we can do that. Come with us, Karen."

The first floor had a living room, formal dining room, country kitchen, and den. Off the den were glass sliding doors that went out to a big deck. The backyard had an in-ground pool with a fence around it. The yard was beautifully landscaped. Karen asked if both girls could swim, and they laughed. When Karen said that she wasn't a very good swimmer, Jenny said they could teach her.

Upstairs, each girl had her own room decorated the way she wanted, and everything was neat and clean. Dolls and stuffed animals covered each bed. Karen spent time in each of their rooms while they showed her their books, favorite toys, and games. Both rooms had a desk and chair for the girls to do their homework. This made Karen happy. Then they showed her their Aunt Loretta's room, which would be hers if she came to live with them. Louie, of course, had the master bedroom.

When the girls and Karen finally made their way back downstairs, Louie had poured some lemonade and put out some cookies. Karen told Jenny and Melissa the story about how she had lived with lots of other girls when she was young and how much fun it had been. She also told them that she had moved from Massachusetts to New York to live with her cousins but that her cousins were moving to New Hampshire. She said that she loved children, especially girls, and liked living in New York.

Not wanting to overstay her visit, Karen said that she had to get back to the city and that she would wait to hear from their father. As she was leaving, Louie's sister, Loretta, pulled into the driveway. Karen and Loretta spoke briefly, Karen telling Loretta that she was very comfortable with the girls. Karen also said that she thought the girls were very smart and extremely well behaved. Loretta agreed and said she was sure that Louie would give Karen a call later that night.

On the drive back to Queens, Karen kept mulling over in her mind the fact that the girls' mother had just walked out the door and left them behind. It was totally beyond anything she could comprehend. Karen was grateful that the girls had a father who loved and took such good care of them. For now, this was exactly the environment she wanted to be surrounded by, a family that needed her.

Around eight o'clock that evening, Louie called to say that both girls really liked Karen and they would all happy if she took the position. Without hesitation, Karen told him she was convinced that it would be good for all of them. Louie said that Loretta was ready to leave whenever it was convenient for Karen to start. With only one week left in the month of July, Karen suggested a start date of August 1. This would give her a month with the girls before school started, time enough for everyone to get to know each other and establish a good routine.

12

TAKING ONLY HER clothes and journals, Karen packed up the rest of her things for Barbara to take with them to New Hampshire. Not knowing how long she would be with the Piazzola family, she thought it made the most sense to send most of her things with her cousins. Leaving Candy and Sandy was a lot harder than she had thought it would be, but she hoped she would see them for Thanksgiving.

The girls were very excited when Karen arrived, and they took her to her room to help her get settled. Louie planned a BBQ for dinner so everyone could just relax and settle down. Sitting on the deck after dinner, Jenny decided to go into the pool. Melissa stayed close to Karen, chatting nonstop about her friends.

The month of August flew by, and Loretta had a lovely wedding. Melissa would be starting first grade and couldn't wait to finally go off with her sister each morning. Getting the girls dressed for school was easy. They wore uniforms and attended a private school. The bus stopped at the house to pick them up and drop them off. Karen's day was always full handling cleaning, laundry, food shopping, and meal preparation. She had very little time for herself, which turned out to be a very good thing.

Louie left for work each morning before 6:30 and was usually home by five o'clock. Everyone ate dinner together, and Jenny and Melissa would tell them about their day. Karen thought they seemed well adjusted, considering all the upheaval that had gone on in their little worlds in the past year, but, then again, Karen remembered that when she was very young, she had taken everything in stride also.

On school days, the girls were allowed to play after school and not do their homework until after dinner. Karen would always go over their work when it was done and help them whenever necessary. After their baths, they had to go to their rooms until it was time for lights out. TV was allowed only on the weekends, with prior approval.

Once Jenny and Melissa were settled in for the night, Karen would normally retreat to her room to read or to write in her journals. One evening, Louie asked if she would like to join him with a glass of wine on the deck. At first he invited her rarely and chatted only about the girls, but after a few weeks, he invited Karen to chat more often. Sometimes he would ask her questions about her life, always careful to say that if he was being too personal, she should tell him.

Within no time at all, the two started to make their little get-togethers a nightly routine. Louie started opening up to Karen and telling her about his life before and after he had married the girls' mother. Listening was a new experience for Karen. All her life, she had been the one who had done all the talking. She could go on for hours at a time telling tales to Mr. Chuckles, Mr. Bear, and Donald. Karen liked to hear Louie's stories and found that it gave her mind a much-needed rest.

Before they knew it, Thanksgiving was only a few weeks away. After much discussion, Louie suggested that he and Karen make dinner at their house. Because both of them were good cooks, they thought it would be a fun project. The girls could make place cards for the table and help with the decorations. They would invite Loretta and her new husband, Joe. Since his parents had both passed away, Loretta was all the family he had. Karen was going to invite Barbara and Len.

Remodeling the old farmhouse was still very much a work in progress. After Karen had talked things over with Barbara, it was decided that Barbara and Len would come down for Christmas. This way, they could spend Karen's birthday with her. Everyone was in agreement and happy that they would all get to meet each other soon.

The winter seemed to go quickly, and before anyone realized, it was already May. It would be a month of many memories, some good, some not so good. It started with Loretta. One of her best friends who lived in New Jersey was coming back to Long Island to live with her parents. Loretta's friend, Linda, had a three-year-old boy and had been divorced for more than a year. Loretta wanted to introduce Linda to Louie because they had a lot in common. As soon as Louie told Karen, she encouraged him to get out and at least date Linda a few times. He was young and should not be spending his life alone. Knowing that Karen was totally off limits even if he wanted their relationship to be more than it was, Louie halfheartedly agreed.

The last time Barbara called Karen, she had said that they were having the grand opening of The BLT Inn on Memorial Day weekend. They were already booked and couldn't wait for Karen to come up and see it. When Karen asked if they were serving BLTs for lunch, Barbara just laughed and replied, "Absolutely."

Surprises were in store for Karen during this month of May. One evening, Louie came home and told her that the pub he stopped at every night was looking for help. The guy who owned the pub was an old friend of his. The barmaid had just quit and the owner was looking for someone to fill in. Louie asked Karen if she thought she might be interested in working at the pub a few nights a week until the owner found someone. He told her that Pops, the owner, paid well and that the tips would be good.

Louie went on to say that most of the guys who went in the pub were friends of his and just drank beer or shots, no fancy drinks. They mostly went in there to unwind from work and to chitchat with the barmaid. All Louie's friends said they would keep an eye on her and, he was sure she could handle it.

Karen had never entertained the thought of working in a bar, but she really wanted to make more money, so she was willing to give it a try. Louie told her to give Pops a call and set up a time to meet with him. He suggested sometime early Saturday morning before the bar opened so Louie could watch the girls.

13

ON SATURDAY, KAREN went to Anthony's Pub. When she walked in the door, she saw Pops behind the bar. "Hey," he said, "you Karen?"

"Yes, Mr. Vicconi, I'm Karen."

"You call me Pops. Louie said you were a looker, and he was right." Karen just stood there and wondered exactly what she had gotten herself into.

After showing her where things were and how to operate the register, Pops showed Karen how to let someone buy her a drink and not drink it. He didn't allow his barmaids to drink on the job, and Karen assured him that she had no desire to do that. He also told her she needed to do two things. One was to take her hair out of the knot on the top of her head, and the other was to put on some lipstick, preferably red.

With hair in a ponytail and a light touch of lipstick, off she went on Saturday night to start her new job. Things went fairly well for her first night, and when she got home at one o'clock in the morning, she was exhausted. Karen was surprised to see that Louie was waiting up for her. He wanted to know how everything had gone.

After counting her money, Karen thought she had struck gold. When she looked at her first paycheck, she saw that Pops' real name was Anthony Vicconi. All she saw was in her head was "Tony Vicconi" and started laughing. Karen thought maybe her sense of humor was finally coming back.

Karen's bar career was into its third week. Strutting back and forth on a wood platform in three-inch heels behind a bar was really paying off. Pops was thrilled because he had never made so much money at this location. He began to wonder just how honest his other barmaids had been. It was definitely a win-win situation for both of them. His customers respected Karen, loving that she was sexy yet untouchable.

The Red Rooster was another of Pops' places. This was his big money maker. It was a topless joint about two miles away from the pub. He had three barmaids to handle the bar and four waitresses to handle the tables. Marlene was the head honcho, and Misty was next in command. They had been working for him for years.

One Friday morning, the first day of the Memorial Day weekend, Marlene called Pops to tell him that her barmaid had a family emergency and couldn't come in that day. She said that there was no way that just she and Misty could handle the bar, he had to get a replacement as soon as possible. Pops knew that the influx of city dwellers coming out for the big weekend was going to be good for business. His first thought was to send Karen.

At six o'clock sharp, Karen arrived at the Red Rooster and met with Marlene and Misty. The place was packed, and the music was so loud, she could barely hear what the girls were saying. After showing her where everything was, Marlene asked Karen what her normal take was. Having no clue as to what she was talking about, Karen asked her to explain.

Immediately realizing that Karen could be a potential problem, Marlene explained to her that they all took a cut from each sale. This, however, wasn't anything Karen wanted to be a part of, and she told Marlene so. With no time to argue, Marlene asked Karen what she drank. She remembered what Pops had taught her: *When someone wants to buy you a drink, make it and charge them. Then, at the first chance you get, switch it with one already set up underneath the bar that has no vodka.* Karen said her setup drink was a screwdriver.

With all things settled, everyone went about their business, trying to keep up with the customers. The waitresses that handled the tables were responsible for keeping the rowdy ones in line. For Karen, the night seemed to go on forever at a nonstop pace. One hour before closing, Marlene announced last call, and almost everyone ordered doubles.

Around 1:30 in the morning, the place started clearing out and Misty approached Karen, Marlene not far behind her. Both with drinks in hand, they raised their glasses to toast her and thank her for helping out. To be polite, Karen picked up her screwdriver and drank it. Then the girls told her she could leave and they would close up as they usually did.

In the parking lot, Karen started to feel strange and light-headed, and her stomach was a little queasy. The expressway was deserted heading west. Eastbound traffic was still heavy but moving. Memorial Day weekend was notorious for being the busiest time for both Fire Island and the Hamptons. As soon as Karen saw her exit sign, she put on her signal and slowed the car down, and then it was over.

Glad to be heading home, Brian Taylor was also driving west on the expressway. He had just got his two-week renters settled into his summer home on Fire Island. In the distance, he saw the taillights of a small car close to the next exit ramp. The closer he came to it, the slower he went.

Pulling off the expressway just in front of the VW bug, he got out to see if the car was abandoned. The driver's window was open, and Karen was sitting there, just staring out the front window. Brian asked if she was okay, and she said, "No, I don't feel well." After opening the door, he asked her where she lived and offered to take her home. Still coherent enough to give Brian directions, Karen was helped into his car. Within five minutes, Brian was ringing Louie's door bell.

When Louie answered the door, Brian told him the story and wanted to make sure he had delivered the girl to the right address. He said he was sure she was drunk and hadn't wanted to leave her on the expressway. Horrified, Louie said, "She doesn't drink, except at home, so she can't be drunk."

Then the two men went back to Brian's car and helped Karen out and into the house. Louie said he would take it from here, and Brian gave him his business card and asked that Louie let him know that Karen was okay. Louie said he would call him the next day.

Karen began to slur her words and looked like she was going to faint. Immediately, Louie called an ambulance, then his neighbor to come over to watch the girls, and then Loretta. The first thing the paramedics asked Louie when they got there was, "Is this your wife? He replied yes without any hesitation.

When he was given forms to fill out in the emergency room, he wrote Karen Piazzola and marked her relation to him as wife. All he cared about at that time was to make sure she got whatever care she needed. Waiting for someone to tell him what was going on; he tried to figure out what could have possibly happened that night. A priest and a doctor both emerged from the room Louie had been banished from earlier. His heart sank.

"Mr. Piazzola, we are very sorry, but your wife has slipped into a coma. She tested positive for an overdose of chloral hydrate. We pumped her stomach, and now it is just a waiting game," the doctor said.

Louie started yelling, "This can't be, it can't be. Someone must have slipped her a mickey at the bar last night, because Karen never, never would do drugs, and she would never drink at work, with the exception of orange juice."

Barbara and Len arrived late Saturday night to stay with Karen. They sent Louie home to shower and change. For the next three days, Louie, Barbara, or Len kept a vigil by Karen's bedside. On Tuesday evening, Karen opened her eyes. When she was able to finally get the words out, she told them what she saw while slipping in and out of consciousness.

There were very bright lights above me and the first thing I saw was my mother looking very sad and wearing a black dress. Slowly, my mother faded away and I saw my grandmother wearing a print dress with a plaid apron. She too was sad.
The next thing I saw was my father, but he looked very happy, in his best suit and tie. When he started to fade away I tried to find Mr. Bear, and then Mr. Chuckles, then Donald, but I couldn't. They were nowhere to be found.

After that, all I saw was the big round light above me and lots of people in white coats looking down at me. I remembered the hospital where I had the surgery on my spine. Everyone there was very kind to me and gave me a lot of attention. Even though I couldn't walk while I was there, I had always felt safe. To me, it was a place where no one could hurt me.. Then I felt peaceful and woke up.

Two days later, Karen was released and Louie brought her home. Once Karen was settled in, Barbara and Len went back to New Hampshire. The following day, Pops came by the house. He wanted to know exactly what had happened from the minute Karen had entered the Red Rooster.

She told him everything she could remember. Once she had left the parking lot, she really didn't remember much. Pops told Karen that he was sure that Marlene and Misty were the ones who had put the mickey in her drink. Because she wouldn't take a percentage of each sale, they wanted to make sure she would never return to the Red Rooster. Pops knew that he could never prove his theory, but he knew exactly how to make sure they never did it again, to anyone.

Ten days after Karen was discharged from the hospital, Louie got a letter in the mail from his union requesting a copy of his marriage certificate to Karen. The latest information they had on file was that he was divorced. It took some heavy-duty persuasion for Karen to finally agree to go along with Louie's plan. They would get married by the justice of the peace, and two weeks later, they would have the marriage annulled. Louie had enough connections to fix the date of the marriage certificate, and that would be that. All medical expenses would then be covered. That was all Karen needed to know.

Karen's one night at the Red Rooster was more than enough to put an end to her bar career. Now she had to put an end to her career as a nanny. This was not where she wanted to be anymore. She had brought a lot of baggage with her to the Piazzola house, some of which she had been able to discard. Karen knew that she was still carrying around too much stuff. She also knew that the only way for her to let it go would be to live in her own place, totally alone.

Because Louie had started dating Linda, Karen wouldn't feel as though she was abandoning Louie or the girls. Louie and Linda were getting closer, and he had already grown attached to her three-year-old son. On several occasions, Linda mentioned that if she wanted to remain sane, she needed to move out of her parents' home. Karen was sure she would move in with Louie and take care of the girls if he asked her to.

After telling Louie her plans, Karen called Brian. She and Brian had spoken on the phone a couple of times a week since the incident, and she really wanted to meet with him in person. Brian had told her several times that he had a place that she could rent in the city when she was ready to leave Long Island. Well, now she was ready. When Louie suggested he would have a BBQ and pool party for the kids to celebrate the fourth of July, Karen thought this would be a good time for her and Brian to get together to firm up some plans.

Brian arrived about one o'clock in the afternoon, and Karen was thrilled to finally meet him in person. There was immediate chemistry between the two. Karen thought he looked like a surfer from California with his blond hair and wonderful tan. Not only was he extremely handsome, he was kind and gentle.

Three weeks before her first anniversary as a nanny for the Piazzola family, Karen was leaving. There was a whole new world waiting for her, and Brian was taking her there. He arrived at ten o'clock that morning, and after Karen had said her good-byes, they headed for Manhattan.

14

BRIAN TAYLOR WAS the head photographer for *Eye on Fashion* magazine, headquartered in midtown Manhattan. He had worked for the magazine for the past ten years and was well like by all those who came in contact with him. His staff consisted of an assistant photographer, two makeup artists, and several freelance photographers.

Living within walking distance to the magazine was one of Brian's best decisions. He loved the city, and when he had first relocated to New York from San Diego, he had purchased a very spacious loft in the Village. The previous year, however, he had moved into an apartment a few blocks away from the loft with his life partner. He kept the loft so he would have a different mailing address from that of his partner for very personal reasons.

The two men could not go public with their relationship because his partner held a position at *Eye on Fashion* that was too high for him to expose his secret life. Brian was happy to rent the loft to Karen because it would mean that someone would be living there full time. He made the rent very affordable with the understanding that he would continue to get his mail at the address and that if he needed to use his studio area of the loft, he could do that.

Nothing could have prepared Karen for what she saw when they entered Brian's place. It was the most amazing layout she had ever seen. Half of the loft was filled with cameras, screens, and props, and the other half was a kitchen area with a bar, comfy couches, two coffee tables, and several end tables. Although the place had very artsy look, it was immaculate and felt warm and homey at the same time. There was one bathroom, and in the back corner was a small enclosed bedroom.

Everything was perfect, but Karen needed a work space, so Brian agreed to set one up for her. He knew where she could get an electric typewriter, and he would have everything in place within the next week. One very comforting thing was that Karen knew Brian was only a few blocks away. If she ever needed anything, he would always be there for her.

Karen's self-discovery journey was about to begin, and she couldn't be more excited. Karen was on her own, at last, for the very first time in her life. The only scary part now was that she would actually have to face who she really was, what she really wanted, and how she would get that. Knowing that she had made the decision to give herself one whole year to accomplish this was very comforting. There was plenty of time.

Barbara continued to support Karen's decisions. The only promise that Karen had to make was that she would call, every Sunday, and let Barbara and Len know that she was okay. Barbara and Len were a little disappointed when Karen told them she had sold her car. Although this would make it difficult for Karen to get to New Hampshire, both Barbara and Len loved coming to the city, and this would give them a wonderful excuse. If they couldn't get together for Thanksgiving, they knew that would all be together in Manhattan for Christmas.

The time had come for Karen to start unpacking and putting things in place. Everything had to be in perfect order before she could begin her new life. She left the box her journals were in for last. Since Karen had graduated from business school, all of her notes had been written in shorthand, meticulously labeled and dated. She knew that once they were opened she would do nothing but start transcribing them, nonstop, one by one.

It was always very important to Karen that she maintain her secretarial skills. Her writing and grammar had always come easily, but to land a job with a decent salary, she needed to be a good stenographer and an excellent typist. During the coming year she could work on her typing speed and then look for a job.

The day Karen finally opened her box of journals; she found at the bottom of the box several handwritten notes that set off several days of uncontrollable crying. The first note she read was *why do good people have to die...how could someone like my grandmother who loved to bake wonderful pies and cookies die in a fire? It didn't make any sense...it was just cruel.*

Then she found more notes. *My mother could never have been a clown. Clowns make people happy. She was bad and hurt everyone. She killed my father, destroyed the Jacobs family, and because of her I had to live in a home. She was a bad person. No, I do not hate her. No, I do not hate her. No, I do not hate her. My father told me hate is poison and it will kill you. I must always remember to deal with bad things and see good things....Remember, remember, remember what Daddy always said: "Karen, you live what you see."* The more she read, the more she cried.

It took Karen about four days of reading and crying to finally decide to throw away all the notes and concentrate on her journals. It was time to start her first book, which was going to be a mystery. She had already selected the title: *The Ghosts of Crabtree*; it was going to be a whopper.

She would work it around Old Man Fitzgerald and include a yarn about the questionable death of both Ethel and Wilma Tulloch's husbands. Then she would add a tall old tale about the crabby old lady with the 50 cats who lived up the street. Of course, she would have to change the names of all the people.

Before Karen knew it, the month of November was upon her. She had already told Barbara that she was staying at the loft, alone, for Thanksgiving and that was fine. Barbara and Len planned on coming in on December 23 and staying with their friends in Queens. They would celebrate Karen's birthday in the city, and she could join them at their friends' apartment for Christmas.

By the middle of March, there was a hint of spring on the way. With only a few more months left on her lease, it was time for Karen to plan for the future. Karen knew basically what she wanted, and now all she needed to do was convince Brian to go along with her plan.

As she dialed Brian's number, Karen's heart started pounding very fast. She began to feel nervous, but it was the good kind of nervous. When he answered the phone, she asked him if he could spend a little extra time with her on Sunday when he came to pick up his mail. She had several things to discuss with him, but not on the phone.

After making a second pot of coffee on Sunday, Karen decided to go over her notes one more time to make sure that she would remember everything she wanted to discuss with Brian. When he arrived, Karen was beaming, and immediately, Brian knew she was up to something. After seeing her once every week for the past eight months, he was getting to know her fairly well. He admired her more and more all the time. She was one of a small group of people who were somehow able to find the courage and strength to follow the convictions of their hearts.

R . P e p e

Once they were comfortable, Karen laid out her plan. First, she needed a makeover, from head to toe. Second, she needed to find a good job, and last, she wanted Brian to sell her the loft. Speechless at first, Brian just grinned from ear to ear, then replied, "You are amazing, my dear. Sometimes I wonder if you have secret powers that tell you when and how to get the things you truly want."

As it turned out, Brian and his partner were in the process of purchasing a two-bedroom apartment uptown. It was the ideal place for them to finally be able to live together openly. There would be plenty of room for Brian to set up a studio there and take all his equipment out of the loft. He also had some news regarding a position for Karen at *Eye on Fashion* that he thought she would be perfect for.

Finally, Brian agreed that she needed to rid herself of the nanny image she was portraying. And if anyone had connections to make that happen, he did. They agreed that the following Saturday, the transformation would begin. He would be over around ten o'clock in the morning to pick her up for a full day of fun and games. Then on Saturday night, he would take her out on the town and show her off.

STARTING OVER

New Friends
The Italians
Coast to Coast

15

TRYING TO SLEEP on Friday night was a total waste of time. Karen could hardly wait to start the remake of Ms. Peterson. She was happy that she had taken her maiden name back after her divorce from Donald. The person inside her had been hidden for years, and now she was about to allow the world to see who she really was. It was almost as thought she had never thought she was worth much until she started living her dream of writing full time.

Although she was pleased with the progress she was making on the draft of her first book, Karen knew that she would never consider herself a writer until she was actually published. This was something she knew was a long way off. For now, she was going to enjoy every day of her journey, and when the time was right, everything would unfold as it should.

At ten o'clock sharp, Brian arrived with his agenda in hand. Their first appointment was to get her hair done. They had 20 minutes before they had to leave, and Brian wanted to take some photos of her, before and after. A little uncomfortable about the thought of having her picture taken, Karen finally gave in. After a few minutes of following Brian's lead, however, she started to have fun.

Alfrado was Brian's first choice of stylists, and both men were good friends. Once Alfrado had finished fully examining Karen's hair, he told her what was about to transpire. "First, Ms. Karen, you are never, never to wear a ponytail again. It is not good for your hair. Second, I am going to add a few low lights to wake up the blond, and then I will bring it up to shoulder length and feather the edges. How does that sound?" Karen just smiled, shrugged her shoulders, and said it was fine.

When Alfrado was finished, Karen could not believe that was her hair on her head. Now the trick was to know how she could do this herself. All she ever did was to wash her hair at night and let it dry. In the morning, she would put it in a bun on top or in a ponytail. It was a very simple procedure. Before she even had a chance to ask Alfrado anything, he was collecting a blow-dryer, brushes, and styling products. After he explained how to use them, it seemed quite simple to her.

Brian and Karen's next stop was at an apartment a few blocks away. On the second floor was Peter Rossi's studio. Karen's mind was racing, wondering what exactly Peter would do to her. She couldn't remember ever being this excited about anything before.

Peter's first words to Karen were, "Oh darling, I am so happy to meet you. Brian was right. There is a stunning model just waiting to be born inside you." Karen felt her face turning beet red. She didn't know what to say. She knew that Peter and Brian had been friends for a long time and that Peter was the makeup artist for most of Brian's shoots. There was no way she could have been prepared for what came next.

First, Peter pulled Karen's beautiful new hairstyle back and put a headband around her head to keep the hair off her face. Her heart sank. Then he told her he was going to shape and wax her eyebrows. Next he would pierce her ears.

Karen lost all color in her face and thought she might faint. Both men laughed and told her to sit back and just go with the program. If Peter hadn't been so damn cute, she might have argued with him, but he was also very charming and hard to say no to.

As Karen sat in front of a three-way, heavily lighted mirror, the process began. Karen's first lesson was about how to take care of her skin. Peter told her that although her skin was flawless now, it would never stay that way if she didn't take care of it. His instructions were explicit, and she was never to deviate from them. These were the new rules she had to follow every day for the rest of her life. Then he began to perform his magic. With each step he took, he explained why Karen should do it and how she could do it herself.

Once Peter removed the headband, Karen's hair fell back into place and looked just the way it had when she had walked in. Peter also told her what colors she should use and which ones to avoid.

Feeling like she was in someone else's body, Karen headed off with Brian to get a quick bite before being dropped off at a nail salon for a manicure and pedicure. Karen had never thought of herself as anything special, but now she could feel herself standing up a little bit straighter. Taking pride in how she looked was the most amazing discovery she had ever made.

Their last stop before heading back to the loft was to meet with a woman named Sally. The entrance to an old warehouse puzzled Karen at first. Once inside, she saw racks and racks of clothes, shelves of shoes, and a wall full of jewelry. Sally was an expert in selecting clothing for Brian's models. He had asked her to select two outfits, including shoes, for Karen. When they were done, Sally gave Karen a list of stores where she could purchase designer clothes at cost.

It was almost six o'clock before Karen got home, and Brian wanted to take a few pictures of her before he left. He thought it would be fun to compare the before and after shots. They both agreed that going out on the town that night would be too much for Karen and postponed it until the next night. Brian wanted to discuss the position at *Eye on Fashion* that she might be interested in, but that could also wait until the next evening.

Karen's lack of sleep on Friday night and her day of roller coaster rides called for nothing more than a bowl of cereal, a hot bath, and lots of sleep. Maybe in the morning she would wake up and discover that this day had been nothing more than a fairy tale she had dreamt. Checking the mirror the very first thing on Sunday morning, Karen giggled with delight. There was no doubt in her mind that yesterday had not been a dream.

Late Sunday afternoon, Karen and Brian left for a leisurely stroll uptown for drinks and dinner. Karen had always loved walking around the city, no matter what time of year it was. It brought back special memories of when she and Donald would come to New York for their Thanksgiving weekends with Barbara and Len.

There had always been something about being in Manhattan that gave her power. Maybe it was all the people and the tall buildings, she really didn't know for sure. Whatever it was, it gave her the confidence to believe that she could do whatever she wanted with her life.

Tonight she was going to meet Brian's life partner. The plan was that he would meet them at the restaurant around 5:30, which would give Brian and Karen a little time alone to talk about the job opportunity he had in mind. Each with a glass of wine, Brian and Karen toasted her new look and all the possibilities ahead for each of them.

Brian told Karen that he and his partner would probably close on the sale of the apartment in the coming week. As soon as that was done, he would start the paperwork to sell her the loft. There was only one condition to that sale: If Karen ever decided to sell it she would sell it back to him. Karen thought that was very fair, and they decided to seal the deal.

As soon as she spotted a tall, thin, very distinguished gentleman approaching their table, Karen knew he had to be Brian's partner. When the man was close enough, Brian stood up, and the two briefly embraced. "Karen, this is Paul Weismann, my life partner," Brian said.

Before sitting down at the table, Paul came over to her, bent down, and gave her a soft kiss on the cheek. "I have heard so many wonderful things about you, Karen. It is my great pleasure to meet you." When Paul sat down, they chatted briefly until the waiter brought Paul his glass of wine. Paul lifted his glass to propose a toast, and the two men exchanged eye contact that sent Karen into a tailspin. She only half heard what Paul said, and after thanking him, she immediately asked to be excused to go to the ladies' room. Once inside, she ran cold water on her wrists *Oh God why now? It has been years since I thought of him. Oliver was just a figment of my imagination. Snap out of it, Karen.* Once composed again, she returned to the table.

Before ordering, Paul said that he would like to discuss an upcoming opening at *Eye on Fashion.* Happy to be switching gears in her brain and getting away from the obvious love these two men shared for each other, Karen dove into the conversation. She told Paul that for many years, all her journal entries had been written in shorthand and that for the past nine months, she had been transcribing them with no problem.

Paul told her that they had just installed a massive computer system in the company and there would be a gradual implementation that could be quite challenging. This in no way intimidated Karen, and she wanted to know more about the open position. It was then that Paul told her that his administrative assistant was leaving on May 1 and he wanted to hire Karen for the position.

16

ON MONDAY MORNING, Karen pulled out the business card that Paul had given her the night before. She could hardly believe her eyes. Paul Weismann was the editor in chief of *Eye on Fashion* magazine. Only one month from now, she would be his personal administrative assistant. Karen could hardly believe how things had changed in the past year.

In mid-April, Brian called to say that he and Paul were throwing a little party to celebrate their new home. After giving her the address, he told her that he was inviting his friends Megan and Frank O'Brien. In addition to being his very dear friends, Megan was also his assistant photographer. Brian was absolutely sure that Karen would end up loving both Megan and Frank as much as he and Paul did. They were very special people.

Paul and Brian's new apartment was exquisite and nothing like Karen had ever seen. Megan and Frank were already there when she arrived, and from the minute the three met, there was a connection that they all knew would never be broken. Both girls had lived their entire lives in a man's world and found men easier to get along with than women.

Megan was an only child and had lost both of her parents shortly after she'd married her high school sweetie.

Frank was also an only child, but until a few years before, his father had lived in an apartment just a few blocks from Brian and Paul. When Frank's father passed away, Frank and Megan had made some renovations to the place and moved in. They had lived there ever since.

After Frank's father's death, they had found out that he also owned an old apartment building in Brooklyn, which Frank sold for a nice chunk of change. Frank still operated the family firm, FOB Investigations, but now he could afford to pick and choose the clients he took on. Both Megan and Frank loved to travel. Fortunately, both of their jobs provided them opportunities to visit many interesting places around the world.

Karen started her new job on May 1. As each day passed in her new job, she found a new and wonderful side of Paul. She absolutely loved working for him, and everyone at the company seemed to like her. Beginning to work with the new computer system was exciting, and Karen could see what the future held for her writing career. Every day that Megan was in the Manhattan office, Megan and Karen would go to lunch.

During one of Karen's conversations with Barbara, Barbara asked what her plans were for the Thanksgiving weekend. Because no plans had been made yet, Barbara suggested that Karen invite Megan and Frank to spend the holiday with her and Len at the inn. Karen jumped on the idea and said she was sure Frank and Megan would love to come.

Once they were on the road heading for New Hampshire for Thanksgiving, Frank asked why Barbara and Len had named their place the BLT Inn. Karen told them that when they had found the old place, they had referred to it as their little treasure. Not wanting to name it the Treasure Inn, they had come up with the BLT, for Barbara and Len's Treasure. The rest of the trip turned out to be one joke after another about the BLT. Before they knew it, the three friends were pulling into the parking lot.

During their fabulous weekend in New Hampshire, Frank, Megan, and Karen had lots of wonderful food and drinks and a great deal of time to just relax and enjoy the small town and shops. Barbara told stories about past holidays that she, Karen and Len spent together and how happy she and Len were that they had found Karen. Megan suggested that she host the birthday brunch that year for Karen, at their apartment on the twenty-fourth of December. Barbara and Len were happy to accept.

After the purchase of the loft was final, Karen bought a large, rather beaten-up, oak dining room table and six chairs from an estate sale. Karen, Megan and Frank spent most Saturday nights together either at the O'Brien's' house or at the loft. When no one felt like cooking, they went out to eat.

One evening when the two girls were waiting for Frank to come home from a meeting with a client, Megan brought up the question of dating. Because neither of them had ever discussed this before, Karen was at a loss for words. Her life was perfect the way it was, and the last thing she wanted to do was complicate it. She was totally happy with her job, her freedom to write until all hours of the night, not to mention all day on Saturdays and Sundays. Why in the world would she even consider dating? "One Mike Marino," replied Megan.

That remark got Karen's attention, and she started to laugh. "Okay, Megan, give me the whole scoop on this Mike guy."

As it happened, Frank had been at the corner deli the day before and spotted Mike sitting at one of the tables, having lunch. Although they hadn't seen each other since high school, there was no way Frank would have not recognized Mike. After getting his coffee, Frank had sat down with Mike to catch up on things.

Mike had told Frank that after graduating from NYU College of Arts & Sciences, he landed a job with World-Wide Pharmaceuticals and had been there ever since. Frank remembered that Mike had been a real ladies' man in school. Even back in those days, everyone had known that he was not fond of change, just variety.

Mike had said that he was currently up for a promotion to East Coast regional manager and would be in charge of training and development for all sales representatives. He would be working in Manhattan only one week a month and will be traveling the other three weeks up and down the coast.

"Fine, you now have my attention. Tell me more," said Karen when Megan paused for a breath.

Oddly enough, Mike had just moved into Brian and Paul's apartment building the previous week. He told Frank that he had been married for a few years but his wife couldn't take the fact that he was never home. He had even bought her a big house on Long Island Sound and had a docking area for a thirty-foot speed boat right off his backyard. He had sold the boat the previous year and had recently sold the house.

On the personal side of Mike, Megan admitted that she had never got to know him well in high school. Every time there was a party and his name came up, someone would say, "Oh, don't bother to ask Marino because he's probably working." Megan also remembered that he never smoked cigarettes and never played any sports. He wore expensive clothes and acted like a snob. He'd always had a girl or two hanging around him, but nothing serious. There was only one thing that stood out in Megan's mind about Mike Marino, and that was the guy was absolutely gorgeous. All the girls wanted him.

When Frank finally got home, Megan asked him if Mike had mentioned whether he was seeing anyone. "Mike said that he was really fed up with the bar scene and would like to meet someone with something in between their ears other than a mouth. I told him I knew the perfect girl but didn't know if she would be interested. I said I would get back to him."

Even though Karen finally agreed to meet Mike, she had serious misgivings about the whole idea. The only thing that swayed her to even go along with it was that Mike would be out of town a lot. Megan said she would arrange a little dinner party and invite Brian and Paul for a little moral support. She said she would call the boys and find what night they were available.

Because the house on Fire Island was already rented for the Memorial Day weekend, Brian said the following Saturday night would work out just fine. Both he and Paul would do just about anything for Karen, and the fact that she might meet someone to date made them both very happy.

Frank called Mike and said he would be there. Thinking back two years, Karen briefly thought about the Friday night when she had had her one night stand at the Red Rooster and how badly that weekend had turned out. Maybe this night would be the one to change her memories.

On the night of the party, the weather was warmer than usual, and Megan was thrilled. This meant that she could open the glass doors off the living room to their patio. Even though the patio was small, there was enough room for two small white tables and four chairs. It was cozy, and she always kept it decorated with colorful flower pots and several candles. It allowed her guests to have a place to chat with a little privacy if they wanted it.

When Karen first laid eyes on Mike, she was definitely smitten by his good looks, but she was just as quickly turned off by his cockiness. It was very evident that he was totally into himself with his designer clothes, fine Italian shoes, and tastefully chosen jewelry. His cologne was just light enough to make her want to get closer. It was almost magnetic.

Karen decided to take her drink outside until dinner was ready, hoping for a few minutes alone to size up the situation. It took Mike less than five minutes to slip the others and mosey his way out to the patio. He had done his homework and knew exactly what buttons to push to open Karen up and suck her into his web.

17

FOR THE NEXT few months, Karen and Mike spent every Saturday night together. On occasion, they would have dinner with Megan and Frank, but for the most part, they spent their time alone. They enjoyed each other's company while still maintaining lives of their own, separate worlds that neither could enter. Mike's world was mostly his work; Karen's, her writing and, of course, her job.

One Friday night while Karen was having drinks with Megan and Frank, they asked about her relationship with Mike. Frank said that he thought things were moving a little fast and he was concerned that Karen might get hurt. He told Karen that he had got a call from Mike yesterday telling him that he was falling head over heels in love with Karen.

Karen told them she was beginning to fall in love with the idea of spending her life with Mike. They had a lot of fun together and liked most of the same music and food. Both were neat freaks and demanded their own privacy. Most importantly, they knew that they would never smother each other. What surprised Frank the most was the fact that Karen never said that she was in love with Mike.

Megan, in comparison, understood that for Karen, there could never be another Donald. Over of the past year, Karen had told Megan her whole life story. Megan also knew that on those very, very rare occasions when Karen spoke of Donald's best man, she went somewhere off the radar. Once, Karen had told Megan that Oliver was the only man she had ever met who made her so excited that she could actually almost forget to breathe just by thinking about him.

After talking to Karen, both Frank and Megan were convinced that Karen knew what she was getting into and that they would no longer worry.

During Karen's many conversations with Barbara regarding Mike and their relationship, Barbara's only comment was to remind Karen never to compromise what she truly believed in. If her writing was ever going to materialize into publishing material, she needed the freedom to pursue it. Barbara and Len would be happy whatever Karen's decision was regarding Mike and their future.

In mid-October when Mike's mother, Marie, was hosting a birthday celebration for his Aunt Mimi, he decided it would be a good time to introduce Karen to the family. The night before the party, Mike gave her a brief idea of who the players were and what she was in for.

"I was only two years old when my brother Ralph, forever known as Ralphy, was born. According to my mother, they were not prepared for him because I was a very good baby and never really gave them an ounce of trouble. Ralphy was a hellion from the day he was born. He was a colicky baby, cried all the time, and broke every toy he was given. When he graduated from high school, he announced that he had enrolled in the police academy and planned to be a big-shot detective.

"After graduation, Ralphy told my mother he wanted to move into the apartment downstairs. The first thing she did was to immediately evict her tenants and cleanse him of all the sins he committed from the day of his birth. Ralphy knew, living downstairs in his mother's house, he would never have to wash his own clothes or learn to cook. He also knew that it would give him the freedom to screw around as long as he wanted, without getting married. If my mother asked about his status, he'd just say, 'I'm waiting for the right girl, Ma,' and that would be that.

"The third time around, they finally got the girl they were waiting for. They named my sister Rita Marie. With two older brothers to guide her, she turned out to be quite the little tomboy. No one messed with Rita; Ralphy and I made sure of it.

"At the age of eighteen, she married Jack Baldwin because she had to. Now my mother was finally going to get the grandchild she had always wanted, even if it wouldn't carry the Marino name. My mother couldn't have been happier, even under the circumstances. They had a big Italian wedding at St. Gregory's Church, with over two hundred guests in attendance. The first few months of their marriage, they lived with Jack's parents.

"Jack bought the first brownstone on our block that went up for sale. Living close to my parents guaranteed them a babysitter whenever they wanted one and plenty of free meals. Jack's father owned a large trucking company that he eventually turned over to Jack. Rita now has two boys, and both of them turned out to be any parent's worst nightmare.

"The last child my parents had was my brother Robert. My mother only named him Robert because she was sick and tired of listening to my father's constant whining about his Uncle Robert in Italy. If she didn't name her son Robert, no one would carry Uncle Robert's name.

"Robert was my mother's change-of-life baby, more often referred to as a 'mistake.' They often told him he was switched at birth. To make matters worse, they told everyone when he got older that he was a total embarrassment to the family.

"If he didn't have his nose in a book or blasting his music, he was off somewhere on his bike. He was a loner, never played with any of the other boys. After graduating from high school, he accepted a job in Los Angeles working for some recording company. According to my mother, he married a floozy that would never be welcome in her home. It was only a year after he left that my father passed away.

"Sundays, holidays, birthdays, or any other occasion my mother deems necessary, she expects the entire family to show up for dinner. Although there is always some kind of food on the table, the main course starts around three o'clock. If you get there late, you are forgiven if you immediately fill your plate and sit down to eat. And that's the way it is and will be until the end of time.

"My mother's rules are never a problem for Rita, Jack, and the boys. Ralphy has a legitimate excuse if he is working, and Robert, of course, is no longer an issue since he took off for LA, or, as my mother puts it, Sin City. Me? I am always in trouble because I don't show up enough. My mother tells everyone that I have more excuses than Carter has pills, but she just likes to say that because I work for a drug company."

Being part of a big Italian family in Brooklyn was going to be the wildest ride of Karen's life. Mike could only give her the facts; experiencing it was going to be something else. Fortunately for Karen, Mike did remember to tell her that in most Italian homes, there was one unwritten rule: No son brings a woman home to meet his mother unless he has plans, serious plans, to marry her.

The day before the party, Mike called his mother to say that he would definitely come to the party and that he was bringing Karen with him. This was the first time he had ever mentioned Karen's name to his mother, and she had a million questions, none of which he answered directly. Mike had not brought a girl home since his first wife, years before. This day was going to be a biggie for the entire Marino family.

18

THE TV WAS blaring when Mike and Karen walked into the house, and all the men were in the living room, watching a football game. Mike made the rounds and introduced Karen to everyone. As they walked through the dining room to get to the kitchen, the aroma of pasta sauce made Karen's stomach growl. In the kitchen were Aunt Mimi, Rita, and Maria.

The first thing Karen noticed when she entered the kitchen was a counter full of homemade ravioli on a bed of flour. There was also flour everywhere in the kitchen—on the floor, in the sink, and of course on Marie's apron. Karen thought she smelled a roast beef cooking in the oven and just assumed that Mike's mother was cooking for the week.

Mike first introduced Karen to his Aunt Mimi, who was sitting at the table, chopping up things to put into a salad. Rita was also at the table, but she was nibbling on cold cuts and cheese to accompany the beer she was finishing. Then Mike introduced Karen to his mother. When Karen handed Mike's mother the box of chocolates, she said, "It is my pleasure to meet you, Mrs. Marino. Thank you so much for inviting me."

After giving Karen the once-over, Mike's mother replied, "You just call me Marie." After opening the box of candy, Marie lifted both eyebrows and nodded her head, adding, "Oh, nice chocolates. Thanks, but it looks to me that you could stand to eat more chocolates yourself. Don't ya worry; we'll put some meat on those bones. Rita, get off your ass and get Karen a glass of wine. Where are your manners?"

Handing Karen a glass of wine, Rita said, "Come on, Karen, let's go to the porch and have a smoke. We got a lot to talk about." Mike had already joined the boys in the living room, and when Karen and Rita arrived on the front porch, Rita handed Karen a cigarette. When Karen said she didn't smoke, Rita just frowned at her and said, "Everyone smokes. Just take one."

Thinking she might just be in a foreign country and not wanting to insult her host, Karen took a cigarette from Rita. To Karen's total amazement, she liked it. Rather than saying anything further, she just sat back and listened to Rita repeat the stories about the family that Mike had told her the night before. Before Rita was done, they both enjoyed another cigarette.

When everyone was sitting down to eat, Marie placed a large bowl of ravioli on the table with a small bowl of sauce. Karen took three ravioli and ate them all. After everyone was done, they left the table and went back to the living room. Aunt Mimi was the next to invite Karen out to the porch for a smoke and more chitchat.

Before Karen knew it, everyone was summoned back to the table. She couldn't believe her eyes when she saw a large bowl of meatballs, plus sliced roast beef, mashed potatoes, bread, butter, and salad all laid out for another course. Karen found that faking eating one-third of this food would probably be one of life's greatest challenges yet.

By the time they decided to light the candles on Aunt Mimi's birthday cake, Karen was ready for a nap. In addition to the cake, there was a large plate of assorted pastries and Italian cookies on the table. Shortly after the coffee was served, Mike announced that he and Karen had to leave. He had a busy day coming up and needed to do some work before he went to bed.

On the way home, Karen asked Mike the one question that had been running through her head all afternoon: "What did Rita mean when she said to me that she'll give me a call when the next load of stuff falls off a truck?"

"Well, my dear, it is really quite simple. I told you Rita's husband Frank owns a trucking company. Their business is to transport garments, shoes, bags, and other accessories from the garment center to various other storage areas. Sometimes there really isn't enough room to store everything, and so Rita helps out by distributing it to family and friends."

When Mike dropped her off at the loft, Karen said good night. As soon as he was out of sight, she went to the corner deli and bought her first pack of cigarettes. When she finally finished her bath and was ready for bed, she decided it was much too late to call Megan. She would just have to wait until lunch the next day to tell her about the deal she had made with Mike regarding their future together.

On Monday night, Karen called Barbara to discuss their plans for the Thanksgiving weekend. Barbara said that she and Len couldn't wait to meet Mike and were looking forward to spending time with Megan and Frank again. They both agreed to discuss Christmas when they were all together.

While they were in New Hampshire for Thanksgiving, Karen got Barbara alone and told her what she was planning to do with her life. Shocked beyond words, Barbara promised not to ever reveal what Karen told her to anyone, except Len. Barbara reassured Karen that she and Len would totally stand behind her decision if that was truly how she wanted to spend her life.

On the morning of December 24, Mike brought Karen her coffee in bed and a vase full of long-stemmed yellow roses. In a beautifully wrapped Tiffany Box was a flawless three-carat diamond engagement ring. They agreed to tell everyone that they had not set a wedding date. Their plan, however, was to be married by the justice of the peace before December 31.

When Mike and Karen arrived at Megan's apartment for Karen's birthday brunch, Megan was the first to spot Karen's ring. Although no one except Frank was very surprised, they wished the new couple well and had a very special time together. When they arrived in Brooklyn on Christmas day, all Marie had to say was, "Thank God, at least now there is a chance you'll give me a grandson to carry on the Marino name."

On New Year's Eve, Mike and Karen announced to their friends that they had been married the day before by the justice of the peace. Because they had both been married before, they were sure everyone would understand why they just wanted to keep it simple. Megan, Frank, Barbara, and Len thought it was a great way to bring in the New Year.

On New Year's Day, the newlyweds went to Brooklyn to break the news to the Marino family. Although Marie was very upset that she wasn't told beforehand, she immediately announced that she would host a reception for them the following week at her cousin's restaurant in

Brooklyn. She would invite all of the relatives and family friends. There was nothing they could say to change her mind; Marie would do what she wanted to do, and they knew it.

19

MIKE'S PROMOTION TO East Coast regional manager at WorldWide Pharmaceuticals became official in late January and brought a very active life for the newlyweds. The whole social scene was another one of Karen's new and exciting experiences. In addition to Mike's many commitments, they also started attending all the *Eye on Fashion* galas that Karen had avoided before she was married.

Most Saturday nights, they still joined Megan and Frank for drinks and dinner. When it could not be avoided, they would go to Brooklyn for one of the Marino clan's celebrations. Karen never ceased to be amazed at the amount of food Marie would put out on the table. Everything went pretty smooth for the first six months of their marriage.

It was the weekend of July fouth that things started to get a little sticky. This was when Marie brought up the big question. "So, Karen, are ya pregnant yet?" Karen just gave her a half smile and shook her head to say no. She and Mike had briefly discussed the possibility that this question might come up but had never suspected it would happen so soon.

Knowing Marie as well as they did, Mike and Karen knew she would continue to ask them the same question every time she saw them until she got the answer she wanted. Finally, in October, Mike told her that he and Karen had gone to the doctor to find out why she wasn't pregnant. He told his mother that they had just got the test results back and it was his fault that Karen couldn't get pregnant.

Thanking God that he was having this conversation with his mother over the phone and not face to face, Mike listened as Marie started screaming. "You're lying, it's her fault. I know it is. Just tell me the truth, it isn't you." As much as he tried, he could not convince her, and he knew she was going to tell everyone that it was Karen's fault that she would never had a grandson to carry on the Marino name.

Things were never the same for Karen after Mike's altercation with his mother. For almost a year, they dreaded their trips to Brooklyn and avoided them as much as possible. Finally, Mike gave his mother an ultimatum: Either she stop being nasty to his wife or he would stop coming to visit. Not wanting to lose her son, Marie made an about-face and finally told Karen she was sorry for the way she had treated her.

The next ten years just seemed to slip by unnoticed. Each Thanksgiving, everyone would go to New Hampshire and then meet again in New York for Karen's birthday and Christmas celebration. Megan and Frank continued to travel a great deal throughout the year. Mike and Karen stuck pretty close to home, as they always had difficulty coordinating their schedules to get time off together.

When time permitted, Karen worked on her writing. The day she was able to purchase a home computer, she began the arduous task of entering hundreds of typewritten pages of manuscript. She did use this as an editing tool, which was extremely helpful. As long as she was working full time and maintaining such a heavy social calendar, Karen knew she had years of work ahead of her to finalize her first book.

Just a few weeks before Karen and Mike's twelfth wedding anniversary, Megan and Frank made a big announcement at dinner. Of course, it was no surprise to Karen because she and Megan had no secrets, but Mike was a bit taken aback. For the past couple of years, every dinner conversation had ended on the same topic: getting out of New York. Mike was the only one who prayed that the four of them were just shooting the shit.

Now it was a reality; two of the foursome was actually leaving Manhattan. Mike and Karen's best friends had just sold their apartment and bought a home in Oregon. Mike could see the writing on the wall and knew exactly what was going to happen next. Totally without thinking, he said, "As soon as you are settled, we'll come out to visit and investigate the possibilities of moving there."

Karen just gave him one of her looks and replied, "Sure Mike."

In early May, when Karen asked Mike if he would go with her to Oregon to see Megan and Frank's new home, his reply was, "Sorry, my dear, you know I can't get away. You go and stay as long as you want. I know they will be happy to see you, and I am sure they will understand why I can't come." That was the exact answer Karen was hoping for.

Suitcase packed, Karen started to smile as she filled her briefcase with her laptop and all the home listings she had printed out to look over on the plane. Gone were the days when she made all her journal entries in shorthand and no one had ever heard of a cell phone. Life was good, and she was happy to be only hours away from seeing her friends.

Megan purposely never sent Karen any pictures of their new house. She kept saying, "You will just have to see it for yourself. You'll love it here." She did tell Karen that the house they had bought was designed by a builder who had planned to retire in it but ended up relocating to California.

Megan and Frank picked Karen up at the airport and on the drive to their house, Karen could not believe how fresh and clean the air smelt. After getting off the freeway, they soon came to a two-lane road. The more they drove, the higher they climbed. Trees arched the roadway. It reminded Karen very much of the little town she had grown up in in New England and of the special walks that she used to take with Donald and George.

When Frank finally pulled into their driveway, Karen could only say, "Do you really live here?" As she got out of the car and walked along the cobblestone path to the two large wooden front doors with stained-glass windows, Karen eyes filled with tears of joy for her friends.

A beautiful marble foyer graced the entrance to a massive open area inside the front doors. It was the living room, kitchen, and dining rooms under a very high cathedral ceiling. Megan said that the builder had told them the open space was called a great room. It was great all right, Karen thought. She could fit her entire loft in it.

There were floor-to-ceiling windows, a stone fireplace that went all the way up the wall, and solid oak floors. French doors off the kitchen led to a patio and breathtaking garden. Outside, through a clearing in the trees, she could see the city of Portland. The entire picture was something that belonged on the cover of a magazine.

The bedrooms were located in a wing off the kitchen. There was a master bedroom and bath with a sunken tub, and two small bedrooms that Frank and Megan had converted into offices, one for each of them. The guest bedroom had a king-sized bed and was exquisitely decorated in soft warm pastels, with a few of Megan's photographs hanging on the walls. It also had an adjoining bathroom with a whirlpool tub. Karen thought for a moment that she was at a very plush resort.

Breakfast was served at the center island bar in the kitchen, from which she could see the entire living room and patio. Because this was Karen's first day, Megan thought they would just go for a stroll downtown, look through some shops, and have a light lunch. When they got back, the three of them could go over the plans for the week.

20

FRANK WAS WAITING for the girls when they got home, and he suggested that they go out to the patio for cocktails. He had a lot of questions for Karen, but first, he wanted her to know that he had booked Jack Simon, their realtor, for the next few days. They would meet with him around ten o'clock the next morning and go over what he had and combine it with what Karen had brought with her.

With that settled, Frank needed some answers. He wanted to know exactly what made Karen so confident that Mike would agree to move to Oregon. How would she be able to convince him to leave his job and family? Why would he just let her buy a house without his approval? Karen knew it was time to let Frank in on part of her secret.

"On our second date, I knew I could never fall in love with Mike. I, on the other hand, was everything Mike wanted in a wife, since he had to have one. Yes, it was true. Part of his promotion agreement was that he had to get married.

"I know it sounds like something out of one of those goofy girly movies, but in his business, it was very important that he be accompanied by his wife at every social function. Therefore, we made a deal.

"First, Mike had to pay off my mortgage on the loft. He also had to pay all my utilities, including phone, so I could live there free and clear. The only time I had to stay at his apartment was on Saturday night or on nights I didn't want to go back to the Village. Since I slept in the guest bedroom, it gave me the freedom to came and go as I pleased.

"The two stipulations he made were, no one was to be told our arrangement and neither was to ask questions about the other's life, should one of us or both of us decide to have one. It worked for me and allowed me a great deal of financial freedom. Mike will do what he has to do to not have me divorce him.

"Also, I told Paul exactly what I was planning to do on this trip, and he knew that it was only a matter of time before I would be moving out here. He had someone internal that he was considering for my position, and I promised him that I would make it a smooth transition. Paul knew that I would never leave him without properly training my replacement."

Getting up from his chair, Frank just smiled and collected the glasses. He said he thought they all needed a refill before he started the BBQ. He realized that Megan must have known all or most of what Karen just told him, and that was fine. Frank loved Karen like a sister and respected the girls' privacy to talk about anything they wanted without having to be included. All that was important to Frank was to try and protect them from ever being hurt.

Old Jack Simon was right on time the next morning and spread out all his papers on the dining room table. Frank had told Jack that money shouldn't be a problem and that he should try find something close to him and Megan because they were best friends. When Karen started looking at Jack's collection, she realized that she had never really told Megan what type of house she was looking for.

Not to insult their realtor, Karen picked out four homes that Jack had selected, and he started checking to see if they all had lockboxes. Before they left the house, Karen went over the listing she had brought with her and asked if Jack could set appointments for the next few days.

The day went by quickly, and each house was more beautiful than the previous. Unfortunately, Karen had something totally different in mind. The following day, they saw the five houses that Karen had thought might be worth looking at. None of them turned out to be what she wanted.

Day after day they looked at homes, but nothing really worked for Karen. She had taken only one week off from work. Her plan was to find something within that time frame and be back to work the coming Monday. She knew that she could call Paul and he would be more than happy to give her another week off, but that wasn't the way she thought it should happen.

The day before Karen was scheduled to leave, Megan suggested that they go down and get something to eat in one of her favorite lunch places. Megan really wanted to show off the quaint little town they lived in, but they had been so busy all week looking at houses that they just had never got a chance. During lunch, they could decide what Karen wanted to do and how long she wanted to extend her stay.

While heading east on Main Street, Karen looked down every side street. Then, while stopped at a traffic light, she noticed a sign on the corner of the next block. She asked Megan to make a right at the next side street. Without question, Megan put on her signal and slowly approached the next block. Sure enough, there was a

"FOR SALE by Owner" sign, with an arrow pointing to the end of Maple Street.

Set back at the end of the road, nestled in a wooded area, was a large two-story gray house. Over the garage, an extension had been added to the second floor of the house. It looked as thought it might be an apartment with entry stairs in the back of the house. Without a word, Megan and Karen got out of the car. Megan followed Karen up the front stairs to a large open porch. Karen rang the bell.

A nice-looking older gentleman opened the door, and Karen asked if she could see the house. He introduced himself as Mr. Crocker, invited them in, and told them to look around as long as they wanted. Karen knew immediately this was the house she wanted. It had character and charm, and she could see all the possibilities that would make this her dream home.

Megan spoke first. "Mr. Crocker, may I ask why you are selling your home?"

He looked a little sad as he told his story, "I lost my wife a year ago, and my only daughter, who lives in town, is moving to the Seattle area. She is insisting that I come with her. In some ways, I know it is time to move on. This, however, was a very hard decision for me. I love this house." He continued, "I told my daughter that I would go with her to Washington if I could be the one to sell the house, not a realtor. I want to know the buyer and know they will take care of the place. My daughter didn't like the idea but agreed to do it my way for one month only."

The living room had a multicolored brick fireplace with plenty of space on either side for Karen to have bookshelves built. From the living room, Karen and Megan entered a large country kitchen that had been completely remodeled fairly recently. Immediately, Karen could picture the big old oak table and chairs she had bought for the loft fitting in there perfectly.

A sitting bench was under the large bay window, bringing flashbacks to Karen of childhood memories of her attic bedroom. Sitting at the kitchen table, she could see the entire backyard with its large, well-manicured lawn, picnic table, and a few flower pots. Farther back was nothing but big old trees.

Karen asked Mr. Crocker what was behind the trees. He told her it was protected green space that no one could build on. It also had a creek running through it, and on certain days, you could actually hear the water flowing. Both women saw the endless possibilities for landscaping the backyard and knew that Frank would be in heaven. His hobby was planting and gardening, and he was very good at it.

After checking out the large pantry, laundry room, and downstairs bathroom, Karen and Megan went back to the living room. Mr. Crocker told them that he and his wife had built a studio apartment over the garage with plans to rent it to a student someday for supplemental income but that never happened. There was an outside entrance to the apartment, but there was also a door to it that they could enter from the upstairs hallway.

Without any hesitation, Karen told Megan that she would convert the apartment into her office, making it into her new sanctuary. Mike could have the master bedroom, which would give him plenty of room to set up his office in there also. Karen would take the larger of the other two other bedrooms for herself. This would leave her a small guest bedroom, and the only time she would have to share the adjoining bath would be if someone was visiting.

As soon as they reached the bottom of the stairs, Karen told Mr. Crocker that the house reminded her of the house she had grown up in. She said that it was just perfect and she knew that her husband would love it. She asked if they could come back in a few hours with their realtor, as she was leaving for New York the next morning and wanted to close the deal before she left. Mr. Crocker looked pleased; they exchanged phone numbers, and he said he would call his daughter.

Once they were out of ear range, Megan asked Karen if she was sure this was what she wanted. "Yes," Karen told her friend. "I have no doubts." The front of the house had to be facing north; it was the one important detail she couldn't compromise. This house was facing north.

"Okay, my friend, sounds a bit nutty, but I am sure you can explain it, so let's hear it!" Megan said

Karen told her the story of a game she and Donald used to play when they were little. She told Megan of the brick wall that had separated Donald's backyard and her front yard. Sitting back to back, Donald would sit on the wall facing west and she would sit facing east. The idea of the game was to look up at the trees and/or the clouds and come up with names of things you could see.

It was easy for Karen to come up with things like a scarecrow, a horse's head, or a bird if she was facing east. If she and Donald changed places and she was facing west, she found it a lot more difficult to see things.

This played out in her creativeness to write. If she was facing south or east, wonderful thoughts and ideas came to her easily. To put those ideas into words, she had to be facing north or west. She already knew exactly where she was going to put her computer in the studio above the garage.

Megan looked a bit bewildered, so Karen finally told her to just forget the whole thing. "It is what I saw in my mind. It is perfect. So let's just leave it at that." They both agreed to forget lunch, and Megan called Frank with the good news. He said that he would get in touch with Jack and they should all meet back at Frank and Megan's house.

Later that day, all the necessary papers were signed to get the sale in motion. Karen gave Mr. Crocker a check and she was ready to go back to the city put her life in order.

21

THE NEXT MORNING, Karen packed her things and was ready to go. When Megan and Frank dropped her off at the terminal, eyes a bit watery, they all put on happy faces, knowing it was only a matter of time before she would be back. Once seated on the plane, Karen knew she only had a few hours to get all her ducks in a row before landing. In the worst-case scenario, she would have to play her trump card.

By the time the pilot made his "Welcome to John F. Kennedy International Airport" speech, she was ready for anything. As she headed to the escalator to get to the baggage-claim area, she saw him, handsome as ever. They greeted each other with a hug. Mike spoke first. "How was your trip, my dear?"

Karen's reply was simple: "Fantastic." She thought it best to wait until the next day to give him the news.

This Sunday morning would not be the same as most. After Karen poured their coffee, she would normally get the *Times* and put it on the table, but not today. She told Mike that she needed a few minutes to discuss her trip with him before he got into the paper. Pushing back his chair from the table, he crossed his legs and said, "Fine, my dear, what is it?"

After describing the house she had bought, Karen told him that her plan was to be out of New York by the end of August. She said that she would tell Paul first thing in the morning of her plans and then she would meet with Brian tomorrow night.

Mike had known for the past five months that Megan and Frank were relocating to Oregon, and Karen was sure that there was no doubt in Mike's mind that she would be right behind them. He told her that he had been working on a transfer to the West Coast but as of right now everything was still up in the air.

Karen had decided on the plane ride back to New York that she would not take any of the furniture she had with her, just her clothing. Her plan was to buy everything new when she got there and have a fresh new start in life, once again.

Mike's only remarked, "Fine, my dear. At least you aren't asking for a divorce."

When she got back to the loft that afternoon, Karen called Barbara to fill her in on her visit with Megan. She also told Barbara that she had felt it was necessary to tell Frank the truth about her marriage to Mike. Karen said that he was his normally kind, loving and very understanding self about the whole situation. Barbara admitted that she was relieved that Karen had told Frank.

On Monday morning, Karen and Paul had a long conversation. He was very happy for her. Paul reassured her that any time she needed to be away in the next two months would be fine. He said he would start the paperwork to get his new assistant transferred as soon as possible.

Then Karen called Brian. They met at the loft, and Karen told him all about the house she had bought and about the studio apartment over the garage. He thought it sounded wonderful and couldn't wait until he and Paul could come out and see it. The next day, he would start working with the bank to buy the loft back and agreed to keep all the furniture, even her big old oak table and chairs.

Because Megan was the artist, Karen decided to give her free rein to come up with all the decorating ideas she thought would work. They both knew that all the carpeting throughout the house needed to be replaced, and Karen wanted new flooring in the kitchen. Painting and window dressings, furniture, and a large covered deck in the back were a must.

Once she had a plan, Karen would fly out and go over it, and then Megan could go ahead and get the contractors in to do everything. The often joked about the fact that Mike thought a screwdriver was a sissy drink only found at the local tavern. Handy dandy, he was not. In contrast, Frank was a master with his hands and could make a rock pile look beautiful.

By the end of October that year, Karen was pretty well settled in her new home at 229 Maple Street. She often joked with Megan about the street number, but then, they both were number people, and even numbers were always best for Karen. Barbara thought it was funny that Karen's new house had so many characteristics of the one on Crabtree Lane, minus, of course, any extra tenants.

That year, everyone decided to spend Thanksgiving in their own corners of the world. Mike was still in New York, so he would be going to Brooklyn. Barbara and Len went to Queens to visit their friends because they were planning to go to Oregon for Christmas. Karen, Megan, and Frank decided to go into Portland to a restaurant overlooking the city for dinner so no one had to cook.

It was mid-December before Mike finally relocated to Oregon. In the end, WorldWide transferred their West Coast manager to New York and put Mike in his position.

Their rationing was quite simple: cross-training. Needless to say, Mike's family, especially his mother, blamed everything on Karen, and Mike and Karen decided they were done with her.

Megan hosted Karen's birthday brunch with the traditional goodies, and Barbara and Len came out and stayed in a local Extended Stay hotel close by. Although they loved the Pacific Northwest, their home would always be New Hampshire. Both of them were, however, very happy for Karen and knew they would enjoy coming out to visit every year.

Mike liked the house Karen had bought as much as it was possible for him to like anything outside Manhattan. He had decided months before not to sell or rent his apartment. He used the excuse that he would be traveling coast to coast at least every other month as justification in his mind. The city was and always would be home to him.

The next two years were very productive for Karen. As soon as she finished all the editing on her first book, *The Ghosts of Crabtree*, she gave Megan a copy of it to read. Megan thought it was fantastic and told her to get busy finding a publisher, which she did. Within the year, the book was on the New York Times Best-Sellers List.

Halfway through the first draft of her second book, Karen's life went into a tail spin. One Friday evening around six o'clock, she received a call from Memorial hospital that her husband was in the emergency room and she needed to get there immediately. As she entered the hospital, she was greeted by a clergyman and escorted into a little room off the reception area.

Within a matter of seconds, a doctor arrived, accompanied by a local sheriff. The doctor told Karen that Mike was now off the critical list and in stable condition. He had suffered a mild heart attack, and with the proper medication, diet, and exercise, he should be okay. As a precaution, they wanted to keep him overnight for observation.

Although Karen wanted all the details of what had happened, she asked if she could make a phone call first. Megan answered the phone and said she and Frank would be there in the next twenty minutes. Then the sheriff told Karen the story of what had happened.

"Your husband was stopped at a traffic light in town, and when the light turned green, he didn't move. The woman in the car behind him beeped once or twice and then got out of her car to see if something was wrong with your husband's car.

"When she got to his car, she found your husband with his head on the steering wheel, and she immediately called 9-1-1. My partner and I were only two blocks away when this happened, and as you know, all emergency calls are immediately forward to us also.

"When we arrived, your husband was unconscious and the paramedics were just pulling up. After they got him out of his car, they gave him CPR and took him to Memorial. My partner drove your husband's car to your home and left the keys under the floor mat in the front seat. That's about all I can tell you, but if you have any further questions, please give me a call."

After handing Karen his card, the sheriff left, and the clergyman took her into the emergency room to see Mike. On Karen's way past the reception desk, Megan and Frank came through the front door. Under the circumstances, all three were allowed in to see Mike, who was looking fairly well at this point. The first thing Karen wanted to know was who she should call. Almost indignantly he shouted, "No one, you are not to call anyone. I am begging you. Please, Karen, no one!"

The following day, Karen and Frank went to the hospital to pick up Mike and bring him home. Mike had a list of prescriptions to be filled. When they pulled up at the pharmacy to fill them, Mike told them not to bother. He said he wasn't going to take any medications because he knew too much about the side effects. Karen filled them anyway.

Mike never told anyone in his family and within a few days was off to New York as he had planned weeks before the incident. Karen gave up trying to talk to him and decided to jump back, full force, into her second book. It was the only way she could cope with the situation.

TODAY

Bear in the Chair

22

IT TOOK KAREN only another year to finish her second book. This one was a love story entitled *Willow Brook*. It was all about how a boy discovered a girl on their afterschool adventures under the Willow Brook Bridge. Just a few months after Mike had his fatal car accident; *Willow Brook* was in the bookstores and on the best-sellers list.

One day about a year after Mike's death, Karen and Megan were having lunch and talking about the future. Megan decided that she was done with traveling and was thinking of getting a dog. The thought of caring for an animal had never entered Karen's mind before. Megan kept saying it would be good for her to have someone in the house with her, someone she could hug, kiss, and love to pieces.

Karen remembered Sandy and Candy, Barbara's little cocker spaniels, and how much they had helped her get over leaving Donald. Then she remembered all the fun that she and Donald used to have with George. Excitement started to build, and the two women headed to the animal shelter after lunch.

It took only a few minutes of playing with two little puppies before they left the place to buy all the necessary things they needed to care for their new babies. Back at the shelter, Karen picked up her two-month-old black lab mix and Megan carried out his sister. After dropping Megan off with all her paraphernalia and her new little girl, Lilly, Karen headed for home with Norman.

For the next six months, both women went back and forth from one house to the other, always bringing their new kids with them. Lilly was sweet and was easy to train. Norman, however, was full of hell. Karen could not have been happier to have him. Both dogs just loved Frank to pieces.

When Norman started to settle down, Karen started to think about her next project. Megan was an artist in her own right. Not only was she an excellent photographer but she could sketch anything. A few years before, she had taken some advanced art classes at the local college. Karen had an idea she wanted to run by her.

Since Karen had written a mystery and a love story, she was contemplating writing a series of children's books entitled *Bear in the Chair*. Each book would contain several stories told by Mr. Bear from his A-frame cabin in the woods. After she had drafted her first book of the series, Karen asked Megan if she would be interested in doing all the illustrations. Delighted to be able to work with her best friend, Megan jumped on the idea.

One month before Karen's sixtieth birthday, the first edition of *Bear in the Chair* was in the bookstores. Megan thought it would be a wonderful time for everyone to get together and celebrate this special birthday and all of Karen's accomplishments over the years. Everyone agreed, and Barbara, Len, Brian, and Paul made plans to arrive on December 23.

Karen made reservations at the Extended Stay hotel for all of them, and Megan booked a private room at one of their favorite local hangouts for a quiet dinner the night they would arrive in Portland. She, of course, would be hosting the birthday brunch on Christmas Eve. Brian and Paul were very excited because this would be their first trip to Oregon and they couldn't wait to see Karen again.

Barbara and Len were planning on stopping in Queens to visit their friends for a day or two before heading west. They had booked their flights with Brian and Paul so the four could travel together from Manhattan. Barbara arranged to have a car waiting for them when they arrived in Portland. This way, no one would have to pick them up at the airport.

The morning of December 23, Karen received a phone call from Donald saying that he too would be arriving on Christmas Eve to help her celebrate her special birthday. It had been 30 years since they had seen each other, and not one year went by that Donald didn't send her a birthday card signed only "Mr. Bear." Karen knew that Donald and Barbara kept in touch, but no one ever spoke of it.

Dinner reservations were made for six o'clock December 23. Karen thought it would be best for everyone to have an early evening so they could get a good rest before for her big party the next day. When everyone was seated and the wine was served, Brian made the toast. She was so excited to have all her friends around her that Karen started to feel a bit overwhelmed.

Unaccustomed to everyone making a fuss over her, she wanted to divert the attention to someone else. She asked Paul how things were going at *Eye on Fashion* and asked him to tell her what was new and exciting. Paul's response made Karen almost pass out. "The good news is everything is going well and we are extremely busy. The bad news is that our senior copy editor, Tim Larkin, passed away this week of—" That was all Karen heard.

As she started to stand up, Karen lost her balance. Fortunately, Frank caught her before she landed on the floor.

Trying to get herself together, Karen said she was fine and just needed to visit the ladies' room. Megan and Barbara accompanied her and, once inside, started throwing questions at her left and right. The old trick of cold water on the wrists worked its magic, and Karen was once again in control.

Back at the table, now composed, Karen said she had something to tell them that she had been keeping secret for almost 20 years. Just a little confused, they all gave her their undivided attention. Karen was now very grateful that they had a private room. They all had a right to know the truth, and what better time to tell them?

"When Mike and I first met, he told me he was having an affair with a married person. As most of you already know, Mike and I were never in love with each other; we had an arranged marriage that worked for both of us. What you don't know is that Mike's affair was with Tim Larkin, and as far as I know, it was still going on right up until Mike passed away.

"Now, could we please get on with this dinner party so this old broad can get her beauty sleep tonight? I need to look my best for my sixtieth birthday party tomorrow, and I can't wait to have Mr. Bear join us....All drinks are on me!"

Arriving at PDX only a few minutes after Donald's flight landed, Karen got out of her limo and headed to the revolving doors leading to the baggage-claim area. She knew he would be the first off the plane, and she spotted him immediately.

As she approached him, she bent down to give him a kiss on the cheek. As she started to stand up again, she felt warmth run through her body. Before she could turn around, she heard Donald say, "Karen, you remember Oliver, don't you?"

***

Karen's birthday celebration held many wonderful and unexpected surprises. Although she had made it very clear that she did not want any gifts, Donald presented her with a beautifully wrapped box and a card on which he had written, "He brought me many smiles. Thanks for lending him to me." Inside the box was her old clown, Mr. Chuckles.

The following day, Karen said her final good-bye to Donald. All that was left now were many beautiful memories of their years together. In the coming months, both of their lives would take major turns, in different directions. In some ways, it was as though the past had become a picture of the future.

A year before Donald's only child, a daughter, married, she asked if she could refurbish 29 Crabtree Lane and make that her home. That way, she would be raising her twin boys, due in February, under the watchful eye of their grandfather. After an accident, Donald had promised his wife that he would put away his skis, at least until his grandsons were old enough to hit the slopes. His doctors predicted that because his leg was healing well, he would be on his feet long before the twins arrived.

Oliver returned to California to pack up his house and get it ready to put on the market. Although he had been offered a position at a prestigious law firm in San Francisco after graduating from law school, he had chosen to open his own practice. His mother had suffered a massive stoke in his senior year, and having his office at home allowed him the freedom to care for her until she passed away.

Standing barefoot on the cold wet sand on Memorial Day, Megan, Frank, Lily, and Norman witnessed Karen and Oliver exchange their wedding vows just as the sun was beginning to set on Cannon Beach.

CPSIA information can be obtained at www.ICGtesting.com
Printed in the USA
LVOW071909261011

252259LV00001B/2/P